Out of What Crypt They Crawl

Out of What Crypt They Crawl

Stories

Jeffrey L. Buford, Jr.

Fahrenheit Books • Guilford, Connecticut

Published by Fahrenheit Books

An imprint of OmicronWorld Entertainment LLC
42 Water Street, Unit 222
Guilford, CT 06437
www.OmicronWorld.com
OmicronWorldEnt@yahoo.com

A FAHRENHEIT BOOKS TRADE PAPERBACK ORIGINAL

FIRST published in March of 2018

COVER ART: ringizzz/Shutterstock.com (ID 185032865)
COVER DESIGN: Christopher Dobbins
TYPEFACE: Georgia

ISBN: 978-09968784-8-7 (Trade paper)

For all of those spirited souls who believed in me before and after the storm. To all writers, poets, storytellers, and dreamers. I share these stories with you for all time.

Also, for my wonderfully loving partner, Patricia. Such words would not have been written without you.

And for Jason J. Marchi, for all your hard work, convictions, and teachings.

Love to All –

JLB

Contents

Foreword

Stories become our children. We often adopt them, teach them, and uplift them as they begin to nurture the expressive development of language; the elements of age-old storytelling traditions rest at the center of each one of these stories. Some are rather rambunctious, flamboyant, and mischievous, while others are soundless, sharp-eyed, and compliant in the whirlwinds of traditional Gothic storytelling. Admittedly, I always yearned to be a novelist. However, I observe the beauty and eloquence of H.P. Lovecraft, Edgar Allan Poe, Nathaniel Hawthorne, and Anne Bradstreet. These spirited and lively teachers paved a beautiful road for all of us to follow. We cut our own paths as we make our way to the top of the mountain, holding our chests, breathing heavily as the darkening sky of truth colors our ambitions. I did not get here alone. The view from the top of such an inspirational mountain is worthy of remembrance as we follow the digital world.

I pondered about this introduction. I wanted to snap mental photographs of inspiration, glimmers of realism interconnected to the sorrowful and stimulating works of those who have walked before me. I wrote these stories for them. I also wrote them for you. I wanted to invite the reader into a world of horror, fantasy, and science fiction without dismantling the structure of the tales as well as the content quietly sleeping at the center of the stories collected here. I wanted more. I always want more feelings. We all want to feel things we have never felt or desire to feel in a sentimental moment of doubt, pain, and fear. Fear and love lie at the beginning of each story, and it was—as my own typewriter will openly confess—a relatively daunting task to write, collect, and organize these tales for you, my dear reader. I am quite certain you are ready to walk among the dead, explore the vastness of space and time, and crawl into a tomb with those who speak dead languages. Follow me. This collection of stories brings together a detailed view of the past, present, and the future, a watercolor, bleeding into one genre and transforming into another.

The evolution of these tales would not have been possible without the aid of those brilliant writers who bled while writing: Shirley Jackson, Richard Matheson, Stephen King, Peter Straub,

Clive Barker, Anne Rice, Neil Gaiman, and many others ignited a flame of wonder and exploration beneath my own fingers and imagination.

I have been writing for many years, although it appears as if the beginning of this work slipped through the cracks of memory; yesterday. There-in lies the beauty of what we all do; we read, we write, and we learn from what we have read and written down with blood, sweat, tears, and unimaginable physical costs. That's why I am here. That's why you're here. The "Crypt" has always been a place most dare not venture, an ominous and alarming stone cathedral where all of our fears wait to unlock the doors of our imagination and take us across landscapes of beauty, darkness, and imagination. I would like to thank Jason J. Marchi for his tireless work and his heart wrenching words of poetry and guidance. Jason, thank you. I know you're not afraid to open the "Crypt." The characters, emotions, and depth will remind you why you wanted to explore the limitlessness void of the macabre in the first place. Take my hand, I'll show you the way.

Blessed be,
Jeffrey L. Buford, Jr.
Alton, Illinois
Winter 2017

Sailor's Woeful Wave

(Dedicated to Jason J. Marchi)

S ailor wanted to know why his mother could not leave. Stars glimmered against blackness above twisted branches of singing trees, swaying in soft summer wind; warm sand softly fell through deep shades of green and blue light. Sailor sighed, lifted his head above the hill, and shook the tiny rocks from his brown hair. His mother waved. "Mom?" he shouted, heated by warm air from his skin.

"Can I ask you a question?" Sailor smirked.

His mother smiled. After carefully placing a thatched wooden basket on the ground, she walked to her son. She knew he had asked a question, a curious boy whose own mind wandered the light on the stars. A humid touch pressed against her chest, moist and sticky from the wind, dancing with abandoned leaves. "You already did, Sailor. What's on your mind?"

Their small, white house sat on a round hill. Its windows glared out at a meadow of lime memory, dimness crawled through the lilies, tilted, bent, and weary from the push of the wind. As the birds chirped, a soft snivel escaped from Sailor. He pointed to the sky. "I need to go home," he said, eyes filled with a fading, darkening sky of evening. The day was over. Sailor's mother put her arms around her son, pulled him against her chest and placed a mother's kiss along his glistening forehead. Shadows collapsed and Sailor looked like his father.

"I've always wanted to go home. I walk along the beach, kicking rocks, shells, and skeletons while making things up in my mind. I don't want to live here." His voice, trembling with fear, was lost somewhere within his mother's curiosity. She grinned.

"When I was a little girl, I used to go down to the beach and wait. I stared at the ocean waves and waited. Nothing happened. Everyone thought I was crazy because I'd sit on my favorite rock, looking out at the waves as they broke and waited. I thought about jumping into those waves. I wanted to be carried off to some remote island and discover a lost tribe of people. I'd live with them and I'd never have to come back to the farm, home. I stay here for you, but dreams fade, Sailor."

Her words skipped through Sailor's mind just as jazz notes flutter against the echoes of a lost piano. A string of melodies placed along a heartfelt inquisitiveness shook her bones as she slept. She didn't want him to know dreams die. They wander into the bedroom at night while you're sleeping, noiseless and supernatural as dreams always leave golden coins behind, sneaking into your ears, slipping down into your soul. That's when everything changes.

"Why didn't the waves take you to the island? What about the tribe? Do you think they're out there, waiting for you to meet them and celebrate?"

"No," she whispered, as her eyes blurred with unforeseen tears. "There's no island, Sailor. No tribe. Just a little girl sitting on a rock, waiting for change, waiting for the world to listen. It took me many years to discover how dreams make you crazy. Do you know what happened to your father? He vanished. Gone. Poof! Never seen again. He dreamed far too much. Now, he's probably sleeping behind a bar in the city. Filthy no doubt! Come on, Sailor. We're done for the day."

Sailor dreamed of his father. Night melted into dreams made of dismal stars, restless breathing in the silence of shadows; skeletons marched to the slow, tranquil beat of his heart as he watched a wave swallow him. The deep blue stillness of sleep knocked against Sailor's memories. He found himself standing on a beach, gazing at clusters of tropical trees and rainbow-colored sand beneath his tiny toes.

He pushed through the bushes, searching the trees for birds and creatures; sounds of all life died as drums pounded against his head. "Ouch." He rubbed his forehead and observed a group of naked women and men walking along a narrow path. They were singing. Notes jumped inside him. They took Sailor to the edge of the ocean and told him to watch the waves. "They speak to those who listen, to those who believe in a greater thing. Always remember that, Sailor Marchi. Trust such words to be true."

Sailor felt his dream moving away, throwing rocks through windows, shattered glass. Sailor opened his eyes. He pulled the blanket from his body. "It's real. It's always been real."

Morning sun captured birds singing in a radiant glow of a new promise; another day to live, another chance for Sailor's heart to beat against his mother's hushed memory. His father was somewhere out there, but he wasn't sleeping on the streets. Concrete could not be his pillow, for his mother often told many tales. Some tales were believed by family and friends, while others were discarded, pitched into a corroded trashcan of false promises and myth. Myth married truth, Sailor whispered as his mother watched him walk to the verge of white foam from a frantic, singing ocean. Salt mist and reflection gathered momentum within Sailor's heart.

He stopped as the water covered his toes. He turned to look at his mother. "Look," he shouted, smiling as all young, enthusiastic boys do when they realize a mystery sleeps in their backyard. "The waves. They'll take us to where Daddy is. I saw them. The tribe! I smelled the island, Mom. The trees were beautiful. The drums. Boom! Boom! Boom! It's real." Sailor saw the wave approaching, a threatening oceanic hiss caught the sky on fire. Sailor jumped into the wave. His mother screamed.

Sailor's mother walked across the sand, holding her face as tears filled the cracks between her cold, shaking fingers. She looked back as her son's body rested peacefully along the shore, silent, still, and abandoned by consciousness. How could she live with herself? Answering a question is dangerous, she thought as she opened the door to their small house. "I told his father the same story," she wept, closing the door to the danger of telling a lie and a truth; the danger of living; the danger of being human.

The Ice Man

I came from the clouds. On a cold, lonely night, the trees whispered, clinging to winter's final scream. Stars circled a grinning moon as the wind caught me. I clung to a bent branch, waiting for the sun to melt my hands. The immense stone slabs above the serrated cliff's edge provided me with a splendid view of the cold, white valley below. I am the Ice Man. The rivers welcome me into their arms as I cross pebbled streams and clusters of wild berries. I have always felt strange; my hands cannot grasp the fresh soil when the sun is high.

Most humans would certainly go mad living in a place like this; a vicious, uncompromising environment, filled with strange shadows, critters and those unforgettable glowing lights. When I saw the vibrant lights for the first time,

I wanted to reach out and touch them. I sat alone on a rock near my source of power; listening to the crackling of snow as it broke against the mountains. The darkening sky filled my frigid spirit with joy as I cannot walk through the woods during the day. I would become a puddle. I remember a long time ago; I slipped through a crack between two stones and froze. After a few billion years, I thawed and ran again, hoping I would not freeze a second time. I finally saw the radiant light of the sun.

The large circle of brightness in the sky frightened me as I quickly pushed through a field of snow and dead weeds. I paused upon a muddy surface, waiting for the wolves to come. They drank from me, howled at the maddening choruses of the wild and returned to the darkness. A mere puddle in the old land. That's all I was in those days. I found myself flowing through the embankments of wide rivers and reached the place where I saw the lights. It was much colder in those regions. I felt comfortable.

My glass-like hands shielded my eyes from the red and purple lights dancing among the storm clouds on that remarkable, cold night. I watched as these lights transformed, burning in and out amidst the blackness of the cold. "Visitors," I whispered, lifting my head to the sky. As I stood up, peering through the mist rising from my body, I felt strange. I had never felt uncomfortable in my home. The coves and streams are my pathways through these isolated areas of untouched beauty. Suddenly, I felt painfully distressed. I questioned the haunting unfamiliar sensation.

"Who's up there?" I asked, feeling small droplets of water run down my arms. I knew I was in trouble. When I get upset or feel deeply troubled, I melt. I typically roll into the shadows and rest with the cold until I feel contented. The sun haunts me as fish swim through me. My life is my own and as I observed the lights in the sky, new colors grasped old ones as a strange shape formed above me. Green, purple, red, and blue came flying down to the ground. The balls of light landed in the snow. I continued to sweat, melting slowly as I approached the gathering of lights.

"You're responsible for heating me up," I shouted, kicking the snow beneath my feet. "I have dwelled here for as long as the trees remember. Here you are, falling out of the sky, disturbing my rest. Unmerciful things not of this world." Whatever waited beyond where the lights rested caused me to wonder many things.

I thought about others like me. How many more were there? People of ice? These questions haunted me as I pulled myself to the lights. My body softened as I witnessed an assembly of tall, pale creatures. Their pigmentation was undetectable, for my own eyes blurred across long, slender faces. The quizzical glimmer in their eyes revealed more than I wanted to know. They wanted to know why I was dwelling along the edges of earth's overhangs, clinging to bent branches and grimy chunks of ice. As they placed me in a small, glass jar, I realized I was going someplace beyond the coldness of home. I remember looking down at the towering snow-covered pines. These peculiar creatures had me trapped in a jar. I was leaving home, and I wasn't certain I was coming back.

Imagine being a liquid for billions of years, you'll understand. The cold air is all that can give me life; I lost sight of all things from this world and my liquid form remained protected by the visitors who had taken me as I was just about to drip to the floor of my favorite cave. I saw the outside of a solid spherical object, projecting the very same hues I had seen down below. Such spectacular colors concealed the external features of the object.

Metallic doors opened through an arched entryway where one of the visitors stood. The others disappeared through a haze of yellow, pulsating light. I was placed on a shiny horizontal table near a collection of pipes blowing odorless, white condensation. One of the visitors opened the jar, exposing my liquefied being to the air inside the craft. At first, I felt all the droplets of water running down the table pulling together; the coolness of the room allowed me to return to my former body. A body of solidity. A body of solid ice.

"What is the meaning of this? I demand to know. I have not disturbed the order of the natural world."

A voice that matched my own spoke.

"There's no reason for you to feel frightened, Ice Man. We've watched you from the skies for some time now and we believe you're ready." The being moved from the door and revealed its features in the soft light from above. The pipes continued to produce cold air.

"I'm not frightened, I assure you."

"I am not interested in discussing denial, Ice Man. Do you believe you are the last of your kind? The last of the ice people who made their way north?"

My eyes examined the being's grey, leathery exterior. Large, black eyes stared down at me as I felt smaller and smaller. I lowered my head to see if I were liquefying again. I was safe.

"I have never pondered about it much," I said. "I walk among the northern woods, watching the bears as they catch fresh salmon from my liquid veins. I know nothing of ice people."

"You are the last one," the being said, lifting up its thin arm to touch my forehead with a long finger. "So cold. I can sense temperatures at will.

If I want to detect warmth, I will find it. The same goes with the cold. I can't believe you are here with us. A true Ice Man!"

I was standing alone with the creature in its own dwelling; my hands trembled, for the cold within my own skin breathed out from my icy skin. I wondered if the creature would harm me or perhaps utilize the peculiar room to evaporate my spirit.

"I have no business being here," I said. "I'm not interested in my history. I wish to go back to my home."

"Have you not thought of the world below, Ice Man?" the creature asked, tilting its oval shaped head to the right. "Do you not know of your ancestors? Do you know what happened to them?"

I watched the creature move across the room, swinging its arms as its body recoiled where the pipes produced cold air. I heard from the trees that most of my kin dwelled in the north, moving through time as I had, holding onto the roots of trees and mountains. The trees began to whisper about the sun and how the heat melted all of my brothers and sisters. Time came through the open doors of earth and the wind changed everything. All of those who occupied the north poured through all the grasslands and swamps; their tears creating the oceans of the earth.

"I have only listened to the trees and the stories whispered to me when I was a mere droplet of life's blood," I said. "I walk through the darkened lands without trepidation occupying my shadow. What do you wish to do with me?"

"Oceans they were, oceans they are now not," the creature said. "They're down there, waiting for you to join them. You have wandered far too long beneath isolation and sadness. Your lonesome soul aches. We all heard it from another galaxy. Of course, we have been here before. Soon, we are going to help a group of humanoids near the equator. They desire pyramids. We require gold to power our crafts."

I listened to the sound of my own voice emerging from the eyes of the creature. I wondered where the other beings had gone, but my mind turned to my home. Because the creatures cooled the room, I did not detect a threat.

"Your people are now holding your planet together. North and south. The seemingly endless white of the northern realm and the southern realm. Their faces can be seen from the ocean, Ice Man. Your people did not melt to become oceans. Unknowing foolishness from unloved trees, Ice Man. Your people have become the massive glaciers of the earth, shards of white drifting on the sea, placid, quiet, and eternally watchful. Do you not desire to join your people? To merge with them?"

"No," I said. "I must admit my heart is saddened by your words. I have been fooled by the trees for the last time."

"Ice Man, the trees do not only fool but inspire. Do not seek knowledge from the trees. They have been talking amongst themselves with their silly tales since earth pushed through the first blast of beginning. The creation of all we know and choose to see."

I wanted to understand the creature's explanations concerning my own people and their evolution. Had I been listening to the misleading words of the trees for too long? My ancestors had given themselves over to earth, to protect her seasons as well as support all of her life. The elements were all changing and the creature wanted me to know just that. I had seen the fires burning from the south, where the coastline vanished in a thick blast of ash and smoke. The earth spoke to the trees as the wind moved across the seas just as waves crashed to asphyxiate the large fires scalding the surface of earth.

The craft moved. I reached out and caught my balance. If the craft had shifted more quickly, I would have fallen and shattered into thousands of pieces; each fragment an eye for me to see the polished metallic floors and walls, the constellations of black pipes and wires running along the base of the floor.

"That could've been rather ugly," I noted, discerning an unsettling melancholia behind the creature's eyes. I longed for home, for I feared the other creatures would return and take me away. Having no true purpose provided me with strength. They wanted gold. Gold was everywhere down there.

"You must be careful. Now, I am sure you're aware that the world below is changing. You have been lost, Ice Man. While you listen to the stories from the trees and freeze as icicles, the organisms of your environment shall not persevere unless you follow the path of the other ice people. There's a balance in all things, whether we see them at first or a trillion years later, all things in motion must be on leveled ground. You are not helping this situation. You've inhabited this horrid form for ages, running from the sun, lurking in caves. Now is the time to see the faces of your people in the ice."

"If I return to earth, what will happen to me? I mean, how will I experience what I do know? The birds? The trees? How?"

The creature waited a few moments before responding. Moments of quietness brought images of mountains and clouds to my mind.

"That's just it," the creature said. "I am not certain you will experience those things again as being in your truly natural form will allow you to feel all motion of this marvelous planet. Can you believe there are those who wish to destroy this planet? Other species from distant worlds, waiting to consume what remains? Protect her. This planet's worth it."

I thought of all the faces lost between the ice, waiting for my arrival, drifting and shifting as the winds touched the floors of ash and smoke. I had been quite protective of the beauty of my world. I imagined the creature peering into the glass hearts of the indigenous species of earth, perplexed and overwhelmed by the infinite ingenuity and magnificence of all divisions of life. My mind, chilled by thought, angered by confusion, moved to the idea of changing my physical form into the ice holding the earth.

"I will take my place," I said. "I am the last of my kind. There will never be another ice man to walk the snow filled valleys of a phenomenal world. What will it feel like?"

"Imagine being loved backwards," the creature said, holding out its pale hand. As I grasped the creature's hand, the ship moved again, swinging from left to right. I managed to hold my weight against the wall.

All my visions of the world jumped across my mind as I observed the ice crawling across deep, blue waters of home. I do not remember witnessing the lights fading in the darkness, only a memory of falling into a circular tunnel filled with snow. When I saw the faces of my ancestors, they smiled and large fragments of ice wallowed in the agitated waters. A welcoming wind blew out from the east and I found my home. For all time I shall float to watch as others find their true homes, too.

The Pushing Machines
and the Chemical
Monster

No one dared to speak. Among the smoke-filled air, nervous fingers tapped against a long, mahogany desk where so many lives had been ruined; helpless mothers and fathers who struggled to fight the foreboding spectacle of lobbyists and politicians gathering along the sidewalks as the Pushing Machines patrolled city streets. Children threw stones at the monstrous engines as they delivered packages on every doorstep in America.

Some citizens even manufactured homemade bombs, methodically planting the little devils along interstate highways and town boarders. Deactivate the Pushing Machines. Such mechanical spies were manufactured from titanium alloy, a glistening silver sheen blinded the eyes of onlookers as they guarded the streets from angry civilians.

They were all summoned to the bad room, the place where people came to get fired or pushed around. Most of the employees had seen it all before. But, Hanna McBride never saw a thing. She had been working with the company for a little over seven months, hoping to climb the corporate ladder. Unfortunately, however, Hanna never found the ladder and now she did not want to. Not anymore.

The door in the back of the room opened. Larry Crawford appeared to be a man of confidence and strength; he was the kind of guy who felt like kicking America in the chest when no one was looking.

Crawford found it rather difficult to conceal his endless receipts from escorts across town. The receipts were printed in Hanna's office.

"I'm fired," Hanna whispered, glaring at Crawford's face. "He's going to throw me out like trash. I can feel it coming."

The gentleman sitting next to her turned and smiled. Hanna imagined he heard her whispers of frustration. She grinned.

"Let's get down to business," Crawford shouted, folding his arms over his broad chest. "We've got a lot to talk about this morning. I'm just going to jump right in if that's all right with you guys." He removed a pair of black-trimmed glasses from his pocket, cleared his throat and placed a pile of papers before him. "Let's see," he mumbled, flipping through the papers carelessly. "I'll find it here somewhere, I promise. Where the hell is that damn thing? One moment."

Hanna rolled her eyes.

"I'm holding here in my hands, a piece of paper that's going to not only destroy this company, but also damage our public reputation. This is a copy of an email. Yes, a damn email." Crawford's voice cracked as he looked across the table. Hanna's eyes locked with the crazed beast at the other end of the table. "Do you know what this email contains, Hanna?" Everyone looked at her; eyes of greed and unwavering cruelty. The institutional white walls with cracks in them were closing in on her as her sweaty palms smeared across the glazed desk. At least the cleaning lady had been doing her job.

"I'm looking out for the peoples' best interest, Crawford. I knew when I arrived here I'd have some trouble fitting in, but I've completed all of our quarterly reports without complaint while you throw parties on the top floor." She felt her pulse everywhere, banging in her feet, drumming against her chest as her auburn hair drifted down above her cleavage. *This son of a bitch is going to fire me in front of everyone!* Her black and purple suit cost more than the insurance on her car. There goes another few dead presidents out the window.

"McBride!" he shouted, slamming his large hands on the desk. "You released a classified email to the largest newspaper in the world. One of the last standing monuments of lies and corruption." He chuckled.

"Lies and corruption," Hanna said, raising her eyes above faceless employees who buried their noises deep in Crawford's ass; they danced with him when music played on weekends. Lines of coke snorted through their fanatical nostrils of insanity. Money. Drugs. Sex. Corruption. Familiar with these terms, Hanna pushed away from the desk and stood up. "You want to talk to me about lies and corruption. Millions of dollars flushed away on your annual company parties which you charged to our shareholders' credit cards! 'Oh, they don't mind'. Bullshit. You signed off on a global piece of legislation, forcing all citizens of these states to fire their doctors. No one's left. We have all the doctors. These machines run around the city, dropping off medications like clockwork.

Do you know how many people died last year as a result of not having speedy access to a physician?"

"Shut up, Hanna. You're making things worse. You know what we have to do here now don't you? Oh yes. I can see it in your eyes." Crawford raised his hands and walked over to a large glass window. Tall buildings with flickering yellow lights winked across the city. "I suspect millions, Hanna. Am I correct on that number?"

She felt the rising wave of anger crawling from her toes to the top of her head. Flushed, she gracefully walked to the exit door and grinned. "You have no idea what you've done. King of all medicine!"

"Your termination is effective as of this very moment. Collect your belongings from the office. Burn all the documents in your files. Leave the case reports with Kevin on your way out. Also, take off the suit. I bought it."

Hanna thought she was going to pass out, land somewhere between the coffee machine and Kevin Robinson's newly waxed shoes. "You're out of your mind," Hanna shouted. "You're a ruined man crawling to the nearest corner, and you know it. There's nothing you can do now that the email has surfaced as well as all the numbers. Numbers of death. Numbers of whores and expensive wine. While the people die, you surround yourself with diminutive followers, taking care of all their personal needs. Piss off!"

Hanna quickly opened the door and disappeared among moving men and women dressed as if their soul had just been taken and placed in a box. Hanna McBride never knew she'd just committed one of the worse mistakes of her entire life.

Her apartment managed to drain her pocketbook, but Hanna McBride never missed a rent payment. The door, solid steel, had been pushed in. Nothing left to lose. She entered the darkened kitchen, frightened and lost in confusion. Blurred, tear-filled eyes would not soften Hanna's heavy heart. She placed all her clothes in a suitcase. They had taken all of her files. Computer gone. Cat, dead. This might be the end, she thought as she pulled one large bag to the hallway.

A lofty, striking man stood against the wall near a collection of locked mailboxes. Cigarette smoke swirled around his dark hair. Ashes on the stained carpet.

"Going somewhere?" he asked, raising his eyebrows as his eyes followed Hanna's figure through the apartment doorway. "You don't have enough time. Like me, you're confused, I'm sure."

"Shut up," she screamed, closing the door behind her. "I don't know who you are. Why are you here?"

"I'm here to be the guy who saves the beautiful girl," he said, chuckling. "No, I'm the discourteous, ill-tempered man who's going to save your life. I worked for them, too."

The ground trembled. Plaster and dust fell from the ceiling. The strange man and Hanna listened as children screamed outside on the street. Pushing Machines. Hanna glanced at her watch. "Right on time," she said. "Medication drops. Do you know every time one of those machines drops off medication at a doorstep, they monitor the occupants of the building, collecting data beneath the radar? Did you know that? Did you know that beneath New York City's lovely streets, her subway tunnels have been transformed into warehouses to keep real medicine? We're giving the people radiation capsules, Mr. Whoever."

He did not speak for several moments, gazing out the window at the Pushing Machine as it rolled along shooting out brown, dangerous packages of death. "I designed the Pushing Machines, Hanna. I know. We're hiding all of the effective medications for ourselves. People are dying. They fired me this morning. I heard about you, too. They burned my house down."

"They burned your house down?"

"That's what I said," he snapped, pulling away from the window. He grabbed her by the arm, down the hall to an exit door. Not a sound. Hanna tried to fight against his strength, but he was far too strong. "You've got to understand that I sent you that email. The one you sent to The New World Observer. Not like they're going to do anything about this trillion-dollar empire. They only fired us. Let's go."

Covered in smoke, the narrow alleyways were filled with children. They stared. They never spoke a word to the two mysterious figures. Hanna stopped near an old church. Its steeple stolen. Used to make cars. Pushing Machines were snapping pictures and blasting through buildings. Explosions rocked the city block. "Who are you?" Hanna wheezed, waving her hand. Breath caught.

"Adrien Meyers. Engineer for our wondrous authoritarian government."

"Why send me the email?"

"I don't know."

"Why?"

"Quiet down. I sent you the email because I knew you'd do something about it. Challenge them. I read your reports on the number of deaths. I can't sleep anymore. I am going to dismantle this one."

Hanna appeared confused until she saw one of the large Pushing Machines moving through the alleyway, blasting through dumpsters, cars, and steel guardrails. Adrien jumped out in front of the vehicle. "Program 357571. All action stop. Code 6787790." An eerie quietness fell throughout the tiny vein of twisted metal and brick. Mission completed.

"Did you know human beings can operate these?" Adrien jumped on the machine and kicked his feet in the air. "See. Not a care in the world. If you jumped out in front of this beast here, you would've been knocked down by bullets, darling."

"Enough. I'm not hiding with the rats, Aaron."

"Adrien!"

"Whatever. I need to get as far away from this place as possible. There must be a place for those who are connected to the resistance. Do you know anything about them? They wear masks and dress in black? Anything?"

Adrien looked at Hanna and offered her a smile. A broken man slept within his eyes. Hanna could see as far as that. "Fine, I'm following you."

"Good idea."

Adrien punched a series of numbers into a pad located on the upper end of the vehicle. A circular door opened. The Pushing Machine felt warm and oily. As Adrien and Hanna crawled inside, bullets exploded throughout. People were shooting at them from windows. As the Pushing Machine zoomed down the road, throwing powerlines across the street as if they were mere toothpicks, a throng of dirt faced children ran after them and vanished in the distance.

Beneath the smoldering fires, a baby cried. Crawford stood at his desk, reading the newspaper, the very newspaper he'd demolish in a matter of hours. The team was there, lurking around, preparing for the building's demolition. Kevin Robinson placed his hand on Crawford's shoulder.

"The building will belong to the past in a matter of a few hours," Kevin said, scratching his head. "They both have escaped. I'm sorry. We did everything we could. The people got in the way."

"How many casualties?"

Crawford's eyes turned black.

"A few thousand. But, we're cleaning everything up. It's going to be a quick process. Now, as for our two little champions of freedom, well, they're gone. Can't find them."

Crawford's fist smashed into Kevin's nose. He fell to the floor, holding his face, weeping.

"I'll have no more of this, Robinson. I want them found. I want them dead. Do you realize we're outnumbered, idiot?! Outnumbered! If those people out there, those starved, sickly people get in, we're done. It's over. Millions of people will storm the barriers. We don't have enough guards to hold them back. Hanna McBride and her wonder boy are going to burn in a fire of their own making."

Crawford helped Robinson to his feet, adjusting his crimson overcoat, smiling. "You see," Crawford said, grinning. "We'll get through this. Sorry about the nose. Have Becky check that out for you. I'm sure it's broken."

"Me too." Robinson said.

She felt disoriented as the elevator fell. Yellow lights flickered on and off as the metal doors opened, revealing a long hallway. As she passed large drawings of young children being eaten alive by Pushing Machines, she stopped and wiped her eyes. The vibrant red and yellow paint illustrated a haunting scene she knew very well. She was a part it. Adrien opened a small door at the end of the hallway and nodded.

"After you," he smiled. "They're all waiting inside."

"Who?"

"Find out!"

Hanna McBride found herself standing before a group of unfamiliar faces; voices whispered above the thunderous growls emerging from the concrete walls. She felt safe. But, the sweat rolling down her neck revealed anxiety and discomfort.

"Here, we have gathered an organized group of dedicated revolutionaries. Not the kind waving flags and shouting into microphones. We make real change."

"Blowing shit up is your only solution. We've got over a trillion tons of medications beneath the center compound. I can see you were all former employees with burned down homes."

They nodded.

"Do they speak?" Hanna asked.

"No," Adrien said. "Not unless they have to. We've been organizing since the beginning, when medications were being seized by local pharmacists and doctors. I recall the FDA slamming private doctors, breaking down their doors and burning their offices across the state. Madness. We began to see what was happening. The higher political powers do not wish to exterminate the underprivileged classes noticeably; they yearn for a long, painful death. An inconspicuous mass extermination. Imagine that. The wealthy can have all the medication, while the absence of medication across the world bleeds the rest out, leaving them dying on the streets, tooth infections, diabetes, lupus, ear infections are now common causes of death. I apologize. I get really frustrated talking about all this. But, I have to."

"I understand."

They were standing in the middle of a large room, filled with boxes, chairs, and guns. Automatic weapons did not intimidate Hanna, but as her eyes moved over to the collection of firearms, Adrien laughed.

"What's so funny? Think I don't know how to use one of those?" Hanna smiled.

"I didn't say a word."

"Your face says it all. Learn to conceal your emotions."

"Working with Pushing Machines destroyed all my emotion. Nothing left but a desire to take back what is mine. We're going into the compound, blowing the top section of the roof off and getting that medicine. We're going to let all the people in."

"Jesus," Hanna whispered, biting her bottom lip. She felt fire in the air. Palpable. One could connect to such intensity with the hairs on one's skin, feeling out the approaching storm as hurried feet pounded through the many ventilation shafts above the overpowering, vibrant light. Hanna felt the winds from the storm.

"We've got to get going. Time to move open the outside doors for the children. When all of this goes down, we can't leave children on the streets. This place is impervious."

A woman with a saddened face approached Adrien, holding out a small piece of yellow paper. Adrien smiled and she returned to the doorway in the corner of the room and disappeared. Adrien's eyes danced across the piece of paper.

"Well, looks like they got to The New World Observer building. Two thousand dead. Son of a bitch." Adrien curled all his fingers to make two strong fists. The rage in his face forced Hanna to take a few steps away. Anxious and fearful of a stranger.

"What happened?" Hanna choked, watching Adrian's veins push to the surface of his neck. Medication's important, she thought, but we're going to fail. They're going to knock us all down and leave us in puddles of our own blood. Blood makes sense to the powerful. It fuels their agenda, wakes them up in the morning and discards the poetry of humanity. Adrian and Hanna walked among towering, dismantled aircrafts, old jet engines and foreign workers. They slammed massive slabs of metal against walls, removing batteries, copper, steel, and rubber from crushed trucks and cars. The blue sky pushed through the clouds. For a moment, Hanna forgot about her home, the place where she built everything. Her cat burned to ashes. It all hit her.

Adrian caught her as she fell. Hanna McBride sobbed for all loss of life. Although she'd seen death daily, thinking about it and smelling it in her own life changed everything. Hate filled her body. With reddened eyes and trembling lips, Hanna requested a firearm from Adrien and she joined the others outside. The secret attack would be the first in decades. As Adrien's shoulder bounced against Hanna's arm, she turned and offered him a smile. "The bad guy who's trying to make up for all his time feeding the machine," Hanna said, moving her fingers along the cold metal of her new killing companion. "I understand you."

"Do you?" Adrien said, watching as groups of people swarmed the upper levels. The red and purple skyline displayed an image of nightmarish destruction, tornadoes of smoke swirling through skyscrapers and factory buildings along the waterfront.

"We all do, I believe. I helped create this monster. I will help kill it."

Groups of people flowed through city streets, forcing the guards standing before bent gates of the Capitol to withdrawal. Hanna clung to Adrien's shoulder as they moved through a darkened hall. Lights flickered as bombs exploded. Children cried somewhere far off. Adrian stopped on a stairwell, breathing heavily, almost confused. "I've got to sit down, Hanna. I'm sorry." Adrian's face melted into a distorted image of horror. The man was afraid. "Killing isn't my game," he explained, curling his fingers around his jacket. "I never wanted anyone to die!"

"You should have thought about that before you started purchasing materials from foreign leaders to build Pushing Machines. Those things have been tormenting the world for decades. Look at you! You're broken." Hanna's words cut through Adrien sharply. Such unexpected words forced Adrian to his feet.

"Let's go." Adrian said.

A man dressed in black wrapped his arms around Hanna's neck, holding a cold blade against her throat, waiting for Adrien to see the light flickering within the steel knife's edge. "If you don't hand me your piece, I'll cut her right open and you know it. Watched my children starve because of you. I know who you are. The guy who builds Pushing Machines. The most dangerous weapons in the world. Give me one reason why I shouldn't kill this woman right here, right now? Tell me!" The man's voice trembled. Tears filled Hanna's eyes as Adrien stepped forward, lifting up both hands, revealing his gun as it clung to his back.

"You don't have to do this," Adrien said, walking closer and closer to the man holding a knife against Hanna's throat. "We've come here to stop all this. I did design those monsters, but I didn't know how they'd use them. I was lied to. You were lied to. Everyone was lied to by these fiends. Killing her wouldn't do any good. She's just slowing me down. So, either walk away or do what you have to do here. Okay?"

The man's oiled face turned away from Adrien and pushed Hanna into Adrien. He pulled her close to his chest. "Feel better now," Adrien whispered. "Thought I lost you there for a moment. Come on. We've got to meet the people. They're all gathering at the compound to gather the medicine. We have foot soldiers on the ground now, ready to take off out west, prepared to provide medications to millions of people. This is a breakthrough."

"You planned all this?" the stranger asked, moving away from the stairs. "You're connected to the resistance?"

"I am."

"Jeez, why didn't you just say so. Come on. I've got a car down the alleyway. We're meeting at the compound. We're making all the necessary preparations for Crawford's public execution. It's going to be amazing."

"Stop right there," Hanna shouted. "That's how this cycle maintains its momentum. Killing Crawford isn't going to eradicate greed or hate or cruelty. You've got to understand this."

"I know," the man said, lowering his head. "I know it all too well. The people want him. We all want him. I know what we'll do to him."

Before the waters of destruction rolled back against the shores of peace, Hanna McBride and Adrien Meyer watched the people of the city take back what belonged to them. In one way or another, Hanna McBride knew the world would finally receive the injection it needed; health. Adrien lost contact with Hanna after the fires of government buildings died down; someone whispered he was in Acapulco, Mexico and others claimed he was a sea Captain off the coast of Alaska, hunting down crabs and tuna. No one knew. Hanna returned to her apartment, but her cat did not welcome her. She accepted the absence of her feline friend. As she sat down in her own apartment, enjoying the soft glow of her own light, Hanna McBride glanced at the cover of one of the newly organized magazines in New York. Crawford's face stared out at her from a reddened magazine boarder. Hanna smiled.

Adrien pushed Crawford through the hot, dry air of Arizona. People of all races stood before him. Sand beneath toes. "This is the man you want," Adrien screamed, peering out at the masses. "This is the man who took your medicine away. The man who sought to control your lives with medications, giving your mothers, fathers, brothers, and sisters radiation pills. Do with him as you so desire. I'm off to hunt in Arkansas. I like boars."

Raised, violent voices drifted along the surface of the sand. As Adrien walked away, leaving Crawford in the hands of the people, he watched as they forced him to walk naked and alone in the blazing heat, no water, no food, no previsions. His frail body staggered on a hill and collapsed. People cheered, but death could not be felt in the air.

"Chemical monster," Adrien said. He looked back, sighed, and thought about Arkansas.

The Demon and the Unpleasant Reverend

Southern magnolias blew against a darkening sky; shadows danced along the side of the windows as the train moved along an unfinished track. The train would stop along the outskirts of Dellville, somewhere between the blurred bayou of tangled moss and branches near New Orleans. She remembered the narrow, dusty roads running along the tilted pines.

Astonished by the idea that the conductor passed the last station, which had been nothing more than a pile of discarded wood and corroded soda machines, Emily paused before the metal door; screeching wheels halted a group of impatient passengers at the other end of the train. Images of red sparks and half-finished glasses of bourbon vibrating across small, circular tables filled her head. She glared at an elderly man standing near her purse. "Going somewhere?" A malodorous combination of cheap cigars and whiskey poured from his lips; teeth yellowed from the perpetual George Burn's impressions and the stale aroma of sweat and weary travel drifted from his hat. "Of course you are," he said, chuckling. "Why would I ask such an obvious question? You're on a train carrying luggage."

"I wouldn't imagine a purse and a backpack as luggage. When I think of luggage, I think of these giant collections of square objects. Luggage means you're going somewhere?" She found herself being rude to a man she did not know and the visible condescending remarks hung in the air. Emily Paige loathed the silence. It allowed the truth to crawl to the surface of things. Dark things. Things no one would ever wish to talk about.

"I'm sorry. I was rude. It's been a long trip. I'm coming from Chicago. I'm going home. So, I'm going somewhere." She felt relieved when she spoke these words, almost as if she had discarded a bag of stones, weighing her down as she walked to the end of the train. She watched as the elderly gentleman offered her a forgiving smile, his face folded like the pages of an old manuscript, turned over and over again. Emily expected the old man to offer her a drink or perhaps caress her long, gilded hair. She was used to being admired on the subways back in the city, observed by hollow-eyed strangers nestled between Chicago newspaper venders and unloaded buckets of trash.

"It's okay," he mumbled. "It's okay. I'm a meddlesome old fart. Well, that's what my daughter said. I'm waiting for my baby. I have two daughters. Things went bad with their mother. Can't hold that against her. There are things that happen in our lives and we're responsible for those things no matter what. I've got enough guilt buried in my chest I could fall over with a heart attack any moment." The tired old man laughed. Emily thought she'd heard a similar laughter in her dreams long ago. Familiarity breeds paranoia, she thought, pulling her backpack over her shoulder and merging with the approaching crowd, losing sight of the old man. Voices filled her head, names, places, unimportant dates and the crushing sound of children running through the hallways forced her calm, pulsating headache to fully form as a migraine.

Her mother threw her out on the streets when she was fifteen years old, a virgin in school; another neglected youth caught by society's sharp, menacing teeth. The cool, spring air soared through her hair, dancing along her shoulders as businessmen and ill-tempered mothers struggled to pull their children along the pavement to waiting vehicles. Night had always found Emily Paige early. A few summers ago, Emily clocked out at the local post office early, waiting for her high school pot dealer, Jane, to come pulling into the parking lot with her daddy's new Ford Mustang. Darkness fell far more quickly than she remembered. Jane never made it. Jane crashed her daddy's car three blocks away from the post office, leaving poor Jane Dickerson bloodied on the side of the road, choking on her own blood as flashing red and blue lights winked against her pale face. They never revived her. She died right there. Emily heard the sirens as they rang in the distance, filling the small alleyways of downtown with normalcy, a suitable sonnet spoken to a lonely friend or lost lover. Chicago's haunting melody. Glued to the brain. Bottomless. Eternal. Maddening.

She checked her purse for cigarettes. They were there, wedged between a bottle of cheap perfume she picked up at some shithole in the wall in St. Louis and bubblegum. The good kind's hard to find these days, she thought, throwing her arms in the air. "Where's Debra?"

Emily Paige found herself screaming the name "Debra" more times than she could ever possibly count. Memories of abandonment came rushing through her mind, lifting visions of her mother to the external world she wrestled daily. Being left at the Rub Night Fire Club was one thing, but to leave your best friend standing alone outside at a train station as the darkness swallows streetlamps is not a kind gesture. Emily watched as the older man from the train opened one of the trashcans along the pavement, throwing pieces of paper in the air, shaking his head as he discovered the bottom of his treasure of straws, plastic bottles, train tickets, and receipts.

Emily watched as the woman behind the train station window disappeared. The lights beneath the station's overhang faded, pulling all the shadows from the street to the pavement where Emily Paige stood waiting for her friend. Worried by the shuffled sound of the old man's shabby boots, Emily skipped across the curb and sat on a bench brightened by a flickering sign: Audiologist. In many ways, she wanted the old man to go away, to find someone else to harass. Was he harassing her? She'd been known to be more than theatrical while spending the nights with her girlfriends, telling them stories from high school and how she gave her first blowjob during lunch hour.

Terror gripped Emily. The old man slowly moved across the street to where she sat, admiring memories of the past as if they could somehow challenge the old man and his alarmingly musty jacket. He sat down.

"You're not waiting on somebody, are you?" he asked. "I've been waiting for my daughter. She left town just like you. Not looking for anything special out there, but she sure thought so. I imagine she'd be here by now. You know what? I forgot. Damn." He slapped his leg. "I forgot all about it."

"About what?" Emily asked. She felt nervous.

"I told her to get one of those ... ah ... ah ... ah ... I can't think of it. Things come and go these days. I can barely remember where my own bathroom is. Can you believe that? I built my house over fifty years ago. Now, I can't even remember where it is. I take pills for it. You know what I'm talking about?"

"Yes. You have dementia." She felt confident as she rested her head against the bench. "How are you able to drive? Anyone looking after you?"

"The real question here," he coughed, "is there anyone looking after you? Why are you out here all by yourself?"

"I was waiting for a friend."

"Waiting for friends is like waiting up for the end of the world. I told my daughter to meet me at my house. Searching all over that train like an idiot. My goodness. Where do you live?"

His eyes moved to her shoulders. Emily saw a glimmer of discomfort in the old man's face and stood up and moved to the curb. "Keep your distance," she said, adjusting her backpack. "I don't know you. I don't know anything about you. You're eyeing me like some fresh piece of ass."

"Calm down," he said. "You're confused. I forgot I told my daughter to take a cab to my house. I wandered out here for no reason. I'm sorry if I frightened you. I have to get home. I parked on the other side of the lot. I'm sorry."

As she watched him walk away, she imagined her own father, somewhere in Arizona or Utah staggering down the street with a bottle of whiskey in one hand and a cutout of the daily funnies in the other. She crumbled.

"Wait," she screamed. "I'm sorry. I've been such a bitch. Look, I've been waiting for hours. I don't think my ride's gonna show. Maybe you're here to help me. Think you could get me to New Cave Road down by I-99?"

"I live a few miles down the street from New Cave," the old man shouted. "If you need a ride, I suggest you jump on board. Not gonna stand here all night waiting for you to make up your mind."

Emily could not imagine calling Jane. She was oceans away. Time stopped. For several moments, Emily Paige thought about walking away from the old man. Hotel lights danced in the distant hues of purple and blue. A sinking day. A lost girl.

"Thank you so much," she said, running to the old man. "I apologize. Again, I'm terribly sorry how I spoke to you. I'm a tired ass bitch who needs some sleep. I've been traveling for what seems like forever. Haven't checked my messages on my cellphone in days." Her heels tapped against the pavement. They approached a red pickup truck. Emily glared at her smeared lipstick in the rearview mirror. Her nose wrinkled as the scent of urine, mothballs, and rust filled the passenger side of the truck.

"I know a few folks up there on New Cave, but I wouldn't say we're friends or anything like that. How long have you been away?"

"Long enough to know I made a big mistake," she said.

The truck's headlights illuminated the bent curves of the road, where old, winding fences ran along the side of the trees; houses stood on large hills with twisted fences. She felt anxiety. It turned on in a matter of seconds, releasing sweat from her armpits, hands, and feet. Her heart tap-danced.

"Do you live alone?" She had to pull something from a hat. It wasn't a rabbit, but it would do for now.

"Yup. I've been alone for years. Haven't seen my daughter in years. When I pull up, she'll come running out of the house with her hands out waiting to kiss me. I missed her."

"Where did she go?"

"She went wherever the hell she wanted to. Probably traveled from one corner of the country to the other. Lord only knows what kind of trouble she got involved with out there. People are crazy. I mean, hell, look at the world we live in." He turned his head away from the road and glared at Emily. "Do you know what I'm talking about? This crazy fucked up world. There are people out there who just sit and wait, watching, listening, hoping to get their hands around some beautiful girl's neck, just to squeeze, to feel something other than the everyday bullshit we're forced to feel every day. I hate what I'm living in. These creeps wait at train stations. They wait for people to pass and move along and then they lie. Do you know why they cry?"

Tears filled Emily's eyes. "No. Why do they cry?" She held back her tears as her voice trembled beneath the force of the old man's frightening expression.

"Because, darling," he said. "They believe there's a guy who lives a few miles down the street from New Cave. Truth is, I don't even know where the hell that is!"

The church stood out from the darkness; an old, clapboard church one might see while walking through the streets of Boston's New England districts. Emily Paige was a long way from Massachusetts. It became clear to her just how far away from home she was when the old man pulled over to the side of the road. The darkened windows of the church pierced bent branches along a path of fallen leaves and old tire tracks.

"What are we doing here?"

The old man locked the door and grinned.

"You dumb little bitch!" he screamed, checking the door locks again. "Do you always take rides from strangers. I'm Reverend Burrow. Welcome to New Cave."

"We're miles from New Cave. I remember the old gas station a couple miles up." Emily could no longer conceal her fear. She reached for the window and turned to face the old man. Emily screamed.

She'd be the last one. He promised himself long ago the frequent trips to town were going to eat him alive, holding him back from what he really wanted to do. Reverend Burrow wanted to leave. As he pulled the body of Emily Paige to the back of the church, he paused as he stared down at her face. No one would recognize her. Her own mother wouldn't look up at such a face with acknowledgement. Her beautiful face would be posted along the highway, blowing in a forgotten breeze, unseen by locals and used to start fires by the tourists up north.

He sighed. The weight of the world didn't intimidate the old man with fat, large fingers and yellowed teeth. He made a deal and she was going to be the last one. No more. How many daughters did he need? He'd buried enough of those girls down in the basement of the church, a rather inconspicuous place to conceal the bodies of the wicked. Reverend Burrow blasted through the back door and entered a room filled with slanted bookshelves and dust. In the middle of the tomb, a large hole absorbed all the darkness.

He left Emily next to the hole; a dark and lonesome cavern of horror. Burrow's smelled the history of his victim's screams. That's where the magic is, he thought as he lifted Emily's body over the hole and dropped her into darkness.

Thud! Water.

"Now, you're home. You can stay down there forever for all I care. You will learn to accept the pain you've inflicted upon both yourself and your family. May the Lord guide you through your path of darkness, for the light is within the shadows, Emily."

He tossed her purse across the room. As he lifted his head away from the hole, a voice emerged from its depths. "Leaving so soon?", the voice shouted; soft and yet thunderous against the stones of Reverend Burrow's hole. "I was just getting ready to tell you that I'm finished with all this. You've had me down here for almost fifty years. Can I go?"

"Now," screamed the Reverend. "I captured you, demon. And now you must stay with me until I am finished with you. How much work have you done down there, anyway?"

"More than you! I'm weary of these hapless souls down here. Women of all colors. Women of all forms. Why did you trap me here to torture these women?"

The Reverend laughed.

"Only a demon can gaze into the eyes of the sinful and feel joy. I captured you ages ago; I wanted you to help me change these girls, help them along and show them the horrors of Hell. But, you didn't. You just sat there. The first girl died of starvation."

"Hey," the demon shouted from the hole. "You're the one who wanted to bring them to me dead. Thought killing them first was going to help. You're a fool!"

"So, you're just going to allow those women down there to walk among you without introduction? I mean, what the hell are you going to do?"

"They don't bother me much. They're ghosts. They really hate you, Reverend Burrow. I tell them how much I detest your voice and face daily. This new girl is not like the rest. What have you done? Mortals." The demon rolled his eyes as he placed his hand on a stone slab underground. Water dripped somewhere from a crack in the wall. "She doesn't have a wicked heart, Reverend. You told me you'd only give me sinful hearts. I should've never trusted you, listening to your incantation and following your candle lights. Now, I'm stuck down here with all these damn ghosts!"

"You have yet to save one!"

"And you are not guilty of doing nothing? Blinded by your own false sense of superiority, I guess. My master's just the same. Well, I did get the junkie to accept the fact that needles are bad."

"Don't toy with me, demon. I'll leave you down there for all time if you don't quiet your uninvited comments. I gave you the chance to see God! I told you to repent! You'll gather soil beneath your mind before I release you. Now, I have a sermon to deliver in a couple hours. Sun's coming up."

"I wouldn't know anything about the sun, Burrows. Now, attend to your ignorant flock. I promise you I will have your eyes in my pockets before all of this is over!"

The demon rested quietly in his hole for many hours before Emily's ghost crawled out from her mind. Her figure appeared before an arched doorway. The hole had been constructed hundreds of years ago by the town, to torture those who did not obey their corrupt, religious law.

"Where am I? What happened to me?" Emily's figure stood before the demon.

"You're currently stuck in a Reverend's hole. You cannot leave so do not make some ridiculous attempt to get the hell out of here. You are here forever. I am here for other reasons. There are many women down here. I wish I could release all of you! I am weary of Burrows. He thinks he's my master. I owe him nothing."

"What are you?" Emily asked.

"I am one of the fallen, darling. Male in appearance, I know. But, I have no gender really unless I demand one. I am a demon."

"Shit," she whispered, moving away from the demon. "I'm in hell. I knew it. I've never done anything truly wrong in my life. What the hell is the meaning of this bullshit?"

"Watch it young lady," the demon said, opening his hands to examine the dark cracks on his flesh. "There are others down here as well. Poor souls caught by this serial killer upstairs. Reverend Burrow. What a twisted son of a bitch. You're not in hell, I assure you. It's far more lively. You're still here on your planet. Your naivety is to blame for your being here, I know. Your heart is not like the others. There's good in you. I am a fallen angel. A piece of light will always live within us; those who have fallen. I could possibly use your heart to help us escape. I have no power down here. Reverend Burrow made sure of that when he trapped me with a spell long ago. He believes he can save souls by killing innocent women, starving them, beating them. And, here I am, the demon." He laughed as he shook his head.

Emily took a few steps in the direction of the demon. "I believe you," she said. "I feel it. My heart feels like it's gone and yet I feel it.

"Yeah, death's not bad at all for you humans. Always thinking about the most horrific things. Life is the scary part, my darling."

The demon worked for most of the night, peering into Emily's heart, watching her as a child smile for the first time and images and feelings of things he had lost to time and chance. Emily's light blew into the demon. The ghosts of all the unfortunate women gathered around Emily and the demon. "Do not come any closer," the demon shouted, holding up his hand. "I am nearly finished."

Emily woke to find that the demon had gained some of his light back and opened the hole. "Go," the demon shouted, opening the back church door. "May your souls find peace. May you return to live better."

Emily and the demon watched as the victims of Reverend Burrow danced across the sky. "Where do I go?" Emily asked. "I have no place to go. How do I find my mother and father?"

"Everything will be just fine. But we have one more thing to do before we go."

"We?"

"Yes."

Reverend Burrow opened the door to the church without an upward glance. As he moved to the hole in the center of the room, he felt someone standing behind him. There, the demon stood beneath the webs of Burrow and his madness. "You kept me as a slave. You are not a man of God. You are a monster. Even in Hell, we allow some air to come in. It is time for you to understand. Do you know why most humans cry?" The demon grinned.

"No," Burrow said with trembling lips.

"Because, they have expectations. Bye." The demon pushed the reverend's body into the hole. Emily jumped in the doorway. "Now, you can remain down there until you see the light. How does it feel?"

The demon walked Emily to the edge of the woods where the sign of New Cave appeared before a cluster of uprooted trees. "Where will you go?" Emily asked.

"I will make my way back into Heaven. I have earned it. I released those poor souls and I have seen the light again because of your heart. In a way, your death saved more than you can possibly know."

The Burning of Andrea Lee Langer

Andrea Lee Langer heard the sound of her son's boots pounding against the ceiling. The morning light slipped through a crack in the window above the warped cellar door. Beneath the dust caught in a spider's newly created masterwork, shavings of paint glittered across the concrete wall where her hands had been tied to an old water pipe for several hours. Her lips trembled as she poured her soul into a silent prayer. With both hands chained to the water pipe, Andrea could not fold her hands together. She did not mind. Prayer never cared for her much.

Andrea closed her eyes as the door to the cellar opened. The radiant sun fell across her frail, injured figure. Bruises of beige and purple covered her abdomen; her left wrist had been snapped as well as her right ankle. She could sense her son standing in the light, a faceless stranger with broad shoulders. As he slowly stepped closer to his mother, Andrea lifted her arm to shield her eyes from the sun.

"Duncan. What are you doing? Please, take these chains off me. It hurts. Do you understand what I'm saying to you? Duncan, please."

He lowered his eyes to his mother. "Are you out of your mind? I know you well enough to know you'll run, run faster than an Olympic athlete on Benzedrine. I'm not taking those chains off anytime soon. Make yourself comfortable."

She watched as he removed his muddy, flannel jacket and placed it across an old wooden chair she had picked up at a flea market years ago. How could she have protected Duncan from nature? He was born wrong; the cunning, violent maniac slept behind his eyes. Only a mother can see such horror!

"Thought you were going somewhere, huh?" Duncan chuckled, removing a steel garden chair from the corner of the room. "I think we've got a lot to talk about. Now, may I continue or do you have something to say?"

Andrea shook her head.

"Good. I can't believe you thought you'd get away with it. You thought you could just ask for something and not face the monster in the end. You were warned a longtime ago. He told you what would happen if one of my parents died. Please, don't act like all this is a big surprise. It's not." He pulled out a roll of duct tape from his back pocket and wrapped it around his mother's face. He enjoyed holding her nose shut and counting how long it'd take before her eyes rolled around in her skull and her cracked lips turned purple. "There you go. Got it! That's how it's done. Now we can get down to business. I know dad died suddenly. I get it. No one saw it coming. I know I didn't. I remember how you looked at me when he collapsed at the kitchen sink. Your eyes did all the talking. You knew my kind were never destined for mortals and their sentimentality."

She watched as he walked across the room to the cellar door. The sound of metal clinking together brought a mild pain to her ears. Duncan revealed a knife, flickering in the sunlight. "You wanted me, mother. You asked for me. Don't you remember? Now, you have to let me go or should I say, I have to let you go." He pressed the blade against her throat and pushed down.

October 1999

Charles and Andrea Langer fell in love like how most people fall in love in cheesy Hallmark films. Their outwardly cliché love story had been thrown around at Christmas parties and high school reunions. Old friends began to whisper about them. Cruel gossip. Rumors floated around their hometown about the strange couple, Charles and Andrea Langer. Charles stopped paying his dues to the masonic hall and Andrea quit her job at the library. They kept to themselves. They moved. They became more isolated and a sadness had settled upon them. Andrea unlocked the front door, pushing her mother's collection of old encyclopedias against the wall.

"Charles?" Andrea slipped her jacket off, revealing her bare shoulders and entered the kitchen. She tossed the car keys on the counter. "Charles? Are you home?"

She heard a distant shuffling. Someone was in the house. Andrea picked up a metal pan, skipped across the kitchen to the living room doorway and raised the pan over her head. "Who's there?"

"Andrea? What in the hell are you doing?" Charles stood in the doorway with folded arms and displayed his infamous eye-catching grin. All the girls in high school chased him down to the point where he had to have his mother threaten the little devilish girls with a baseball bat. Why Charles Langer decided to fall in love with Andrea was beyond her own wildest dreams.

Charles reached out and took the pan from Andrea's hands. "Jesus Christ. I know we can't afford another trip to the hospital, honey. Are you okay?"

"I'm fine. I think. I'm still recovering from the news. Doctors make you feel like you're walking on sunshine one minute and walking through the gates of hell the next."

She could never hold back her tears. Her mother had the ability to blink her tears away without a problem. Charles wrapped his arms around Andrea's body.

"Don't worry. We'll always have each other. Having a baby is the greatest thing in this whole fucked up world. I know something good will come out of all this."

"You're too hopeful," she said, wiping another tear from her eye. "Always hoping for the best. It's like you've mastered the fine art of not giving a flying shit about anything. I can't have children, Charles! I can't bring life into this world and it kills me. It brings me so much pain I'm unable to breathe at times." Andrea sighed as she ran her fingers through her hair. "You're just too hopeful. Hope is a dangerous thing."

"Honey, come on. You can't just dismiss the possibility of a miracle. You have to believe that things can get better. What else can you do but hope?" They pressed their bodies together in the autumn glow of evening, bleeding on the inside, screaming at the cruelty of life's irony. Both

Charles and Andrea wept in their own isolated way.

On a cold autumn night, The Listener came to the door of Charles and Andrea Langer. The Listener had grown weary of their cries and sadness. His skin was like ice, a body made from stone and wood like an ancient being from a time when the living and the dead battled the forces of the underworld. The Listener carried with him an infant boy, crafted from the bones of his brothers who had fallen when Heaven mourned, or so he was told. With the child in their life, the Langer's would certainly quiet their sobs and The Listener could return to the woods and continue his mischievous ways. Charles heard the knock on the front door. Andrea jumped.

"Who could that be? It's late," Charles snapped.

When the door opened, the darkness pushed a figure through. The Listener stood before Charles; fingers like branches scrapping against the sky. Soft blue veins pulled to the surface of The Listener's pale, icy flesh. Andrea jumped from the sofa and threw her arms around her husband's waist. "Who are you? What do you want?" Andrea screamed.

"I've come to silence you. Your turmoil has disturbed me and I cannot continue my affairs while you're weeping day and night. I have lived here longer than the trees outside. Tonight, I give you this child. In return, you shall remain silent and content."

Andrea's eyes followed the white mist rising from The Listener's hands. Her heart, filled with fear and warmth from the sound of a screaming child, beat like a drum as she gazed into the eyes of The Listener's gift. She could not pull away from Charles. She wanted to run away and exit out the back door, but she was being pulled closer and closer to the infant. With a broken heart, Andrea reached out and pressed the child against her chest. She slid her hand along his soft, bald head and smiled.

"We can't take this kid," Charles shouted, raising his arms in the air. "We don't know who you are or whose child that is. This isn't happening."

"Oh, it is. You see, Mr. Langer, I am not of this world. I do not understand your monotonous fits and your wife's unending cries and sobs. Enough is enough. You want a child, here he is. He is not mortal. He was made from the bones of..."

Charles lifted his arm and placed his hand against The Listener's chest. He could not detect the drumming of life beneath the stranger's own bones. "If we take this child, you'll leave us? You'll go away."

The Listener began to chuckle. "I have much to attend to, Mr. Langer. I have a couple on the other side of town that's got a fresh one. A beauty. I have to deal with her before the end of the month. You two have been distracting me. Now, I can be on my way and finish my business in the woods."

"This is insane," Andrea whispered, looking down at the child's fat cheeks. She wanted to squeeze them. "I don't understand any of this. But, we'll be given the chance to raise him, Charles. We'll be able to watch him grow and go to school and...I...believe we should take him."

"You've got to be kidding me, Andrea. Some ominous looking man comes to our door and throws a baby at us because he wants us to shut up about the fact we can't have children."

Andrea's tear-filled eyes reflected a sorrow most people discover on trips to third world countries. The misery and sadness were there without decomposing buildings and garbage in the background of her pupils.

"That's right, Charles. That's right. If you don't want him, I'll raise him myself. Please, darling. Please. I beg you."

The Listener lowered his head and whispered, "And so it is. Alas, I must confess if one of you dies, the child will transform. He'll return to his natural self. It takes two mortals to raise these beings. Mortals are not meant to carry these beings through life, for they are too weak and dangerously naive. Fortunately, however, it shall bring comfort to your hearts. When one of you dies, you'll wish you hadn't. That's the way it works."

Charles felt the heat from his reddened face; fiery rage and confusion dominated his ordinarily composed and complacent demeanor. He reached out and gently touched his wife's face and smiled. "If this is what you want, I have to allow it. I'm not sure how we're going to explain this to our family and friends." Charles could see the anger growing in Andrea's eyes. She swung her head to one side, puckered her lips and disappeared into the living room with the child. The baby fell silent; Andrea rested her head against the sofa and glared across the room to the doorway where her husband and the mysterious stranger stood.

"Long ago, when the world was young and colorful, beings walked through the woods, inhabiting caves, screaming at the beauty of the night. When the light faded, the trumpets of horror pounded against the skulls of all those who had fallen. We are the fallen ones, forever lost and always listening. Your home was built upon their ground." He pointed his finger in the direction of town. "This is my home, my place of dwelling. Here, on this night, I warn you that your only enemy now is death."

The Listener quickly recoiled, returning to the darkness outside, leaving Charles and Andrea with the sinister child who did not have a name, an undocumented creature, born from the night. Charles slammed the door and sighed.

"What in the hell are we gonna to do now? We're gonna have to keep him somewhere out of sight. We've got to hide him. Put him away!" Charles armpits were sweating. "This can't be happening to us. This isn't real. None of this is real. We're being tricked."

"All we've ever wanted was a child, Charles. Now, we've got one. What are you complaining about? We're going to raise this child and love him just as your mother loved you. Understand?" Andrea clenched her fists as the baby squirmed in her arms.

Charles shrugged.

He appeared to be broken in Andrea's eyes, a lost man who could no longer find his way in the world. The windows in the house were tall and dark. The wooden floorboards moaned as the wind outside pressed alongside the old framework Andrea's father had built decades ago. It became clear to both Charles and Andrea that they were living on sacred ground, sacred to those who did not lift their eyes to the Heavens. Andrea had seen shadows dancing in the night near the woods for most of her childhood. After erasing the figures from her mind, she began to sink deeper and deeper into a world filled with sleepless nights, prescription medication, and long, dreary walks across the countryside.

"My family has lived here for ages," Andrea said. "I've never thought we were alone on this property."

"That's obvious," Charles said. "I just want to know how we're going to explain this all to our family and friends. I mean, Andrea, they'll want to know what the hell is going on."

"What family, Charles? Huh? What friends? Do you seriously believe we have friends, people who care about us, nurture us, protect us? No. We don't have any friends and I'm rather comfortable with that. Now, if you feel the need to run your mouth about this situation then go right ahead and cause a shit storm. I'm not giving you shelter, Charles. No more." Andrea carried the baby to the stairs. The soft, orange glow from the candles placed along the wall brightened Andrea's auburn hair. She kissed the baby's forehead and offered him a big smile. "Duncan," she whispered, wiping an unexpected tear from her eye. "That's what I'll call you. You look like a Duncan, anyway. Charles, I'm going to bed. You can sit down here and sulk all you'd like. I'm not participating. You were the one who told me not to question the possibility of a miracle. Here it is. Goodnight." Andrea vanished up the stairs, carrying with her the future of their family, a mystery wrapped in white cotton; a mystery that only weighed seven pounds.

Their eyes were glued to the baby at the end of the bed, breathing softly in the dark. Charles lit a cigarette and blew a smoke ring into the shadows. He wanted to love the small critter, but he felt lost. He asked himself if he could ever love a child whose blood did not flow in his veins. "This is a confusing situation," he said. "I don't know what to do."

Andrea turned over and pulled the blanket to her chin. "This is our chance to raise a child. We love him. We take care of ourselves for him. We can't allow anything to happen to us."

"That's what's scaring me. What is his true nature? I don't think we'll ever know, but I can promise you that I'll do my part. It's going to take time. Time to get used to this child."

"I know," Andrea said. "I know."

It took many years for Charles to love Duncan. He grew rather quickly, standing on chairs and jumping up and down for boxes of cereal and slapping makeup on his face for Halloween. The Langer family did not speak about where Duncan had come from. He existed silently with them. As Duncan aged, Andrea noticed how her son's eyes changed. They had been dark, but never black. His quietness disturbed Andrea and Charles. On Duncan's thirteenth birthday, he revealed more than a child's buried rage. Charles hadn't been feeling well; he had been sleeping alone on the couch when Andrea pulled Duncan's birthday cake from the oven.

"Perfect," she said. "That's beautiful."

Duncan was outside throwing chestnuts over the mailbox. Andrea bounced around the kitchen, collecting empty soda cups and cans of silly string from the basket placed on the microwave. Duncan wanted a small party. His spiritedness faded throughout the day. Andrea shook Charles as he snored.

"Charles," Andrea whispered. "Time for cake. We're going to open presents soon and I'd like Duncan to see what we got him. He's going to love it."

Charles moaned. His hair, disheveled and unconditioned, stood up as if a balloon had been rubbed against the top of his head. "Fine. I'm getting up. Let me guess, no one's coming from school. I'll tell you why no one's coming from Duncan's school. He's a weirdo. I'm sure he freaks people out all the time, Andrea. Do you ever watch him stare out the windows with that blank, stupid look? It pisses me off."

Andrea remembered the darkness in Duncan's eyes when he'd stand near the front windows, gazing, lost in some memory shared with the woods outside. Charles often wondered if The Listener would ever return, turning the lock on the door and breaking the door down. Bang! Bang! Bang! The terror followed Charles through his dreams.

"Charles. I'd wish you'd knock it off. I've grown tired of your snide remarks about Duncan. He's trying to adjust to school. You know he's not the most personable person in the world, which..."

Charles slammed his hand against the table, Andrea jumped. She gripped her chest. "You scared the shit out of me, Charles. What's the deal? You want me to go along with your verbal abuse? You want me to be some kind of silent, obedient wife who'll serve you? I'll get you a bell next week."

Charles wanted to reach out and grab Andrea's wrist, to feel the warmth of her flesh, to feel the rise of burning sensual electricity he'd always found to be one of Andrea's special gifts. He missed her touch. He thought about Duncan. Chestnuts flew through the air. Charles clenched his fists.

"I don't expect you to do anything you don't want to do, honey. I mean it. I just wish you'd understand how worried I am. What if something terrible happens to one of us? What'll happen to Duncan? Will he grow horns, develop horrid skin rashes and speak in Latin? I'm trying to mend my concerns. It's been thirteen years since that gauntly intruder left Duncan with us. Now, he's staring at the woods. The very same woods where The Listener walks. No way. I feel bad about all this."

Andrea's fingers skipped along the back of her husband's neck. She could feel his sorrow; he hadn't been touched in a longtime. Duncan dominated nearly every aspect of their lives. Charles visited the doctor weekly, coming up with bizarre medical conclusions to drive his doctor insane. Andrea enjoyed the clinic outside town. They never asked many questions, and the lights were low and faint. They wanted to be healthy. They both knew how important it was for them to stay alive and protect Duncan from his true nature. The words spoken by The Listener haunted Charles and Andrea. Outside along the narrowly cut path winding through the wheat fields, Andrea watched as Duncan approached the porch. He was carrying something.

"Here, mom," Duncan said, slamming the door as he kicked the dirt off his feet. "What do you think of this? Found it down by the stream. Can I go into the woods? I'd love to explore them. See what kind of creatures I can find. Wouldn't that be awesome?!" Duncan scooped a chunk of icing from the side of his birthday cake. "Yum. Now, that's a good cake." After placing a dead raven on top of his cake, Duncan smirked at his father. "Oh yeah. That makes all the difference wouldn't you say, Charles?"

Andrea dropped a plate of blue and yellow cupcakes. The raven's dead eyes stared out the window, almost as if the bird had been looking beyond Andrea, seeking out the shadows in the woods. "What have you done? Duncan, what have you done?" Andrea's voice filled the house. The high ceilings contained even the subtlest sounds and amplified them.

Charles lunged from his chair and grabbed Duncan by the throat. He slammed his body against the pantry door. "You little son of a bitch. Your mother's been working on your birthday cake for hours and this is how you show her your appreciation. You little prick. Here, have a taste of your bird cake you rotten shit." Charles smashed a handful of cake into Duncan's mouth. He wanted his son to have more. More cake. Andrea fell over and covered her mouth. A muffled scream escaped through the cracks in her fingers. "Disrespectful," Charles shouted, spitting in Duncan's face. Black feathers drifted through the air. "If I ever find you disrespecting your mother again, so help me God I'll choke you until your eyeballs pop out of your head. Do you understand me?"

Duncan smiled. It had been one of those chilling smiles, careless, bored, and mocking. Charles shook him. Duncan opened his mouth and vomited on the floor. "Clean that up," Duncan said. "I'm going birdwatching." Duncan opened the door, turned around to send his parents a disturbing smile, and skipped off down the path and faded into the evening sun.

They sat in silence for several hours, listening to the clock down the hall, wiping their sweaty hands together as they fought an unsettling fear. Things were not right with their son. Duncan was changing. Andrea looked out the window where the reflection of the cake and dead bird haunted her. She turned away. "I think it's just a phase, I don't know. I thought one of us would have to die for his soul to turn sour." Andrea's words did not comfort Charles.

"We're his parents. We have the right to protect him. Do we have the right to protect ourselves, Andrea? What if he decides to do something outrageous to himself or us? What if we're sleeping and he's standing over us? What then?"

"Enough!" Andrea screamed. "We've lived with that boy for thirteen years. We've watched him grown. Socially awkward? Yes! Homicidal? No! He's been the sweetest little man I've ever seen. You just have to understand he's going through puberty. We all know how stressful those times are. Hair starts popping out in places you'd never imagine. Your voice changes.

It's all a very discomforting experience. We have to support him."

The raven had been buried outside by Andrea's rose garden; Charles cursed the boy as he placed a small gardening shovel inside his bucket of broken brushes and rulers. "One day, he's going to burn the house down with all of us in it." No gifts were opened that night. Duncan slept in his room while his parents struggled to sleep. They would fight sleep every night after Duncan's weirdly inappropriate assault on his own birthday cake. No one would ever speak of the raven and the birthday cake again.

Duncan remained rather quiet and submissive as the days blurred together through the eyes of two deeply unhappy people. Charles and Andrea dismissed Duncan from school. Andrea slapped a pile of papers on his lap. His shirt was covered with mustard. His pimpled face appeared to have been attacked with an ice pick or someone had attempted to put out a fire on his face with one. No one was quite sure. His voice deepened.

"You're going to have all of these chapters read by tomorrow. No questions asked. Home schooling is the best option for you at this point in time. So, read the first chapter aloud."

Duncan cleared his throat. "There once was a boy who lived with his parents. He was a good boy. One day, the boy found out he didn't come from his parents. The boy came from the woods. The boy came from the woods...the boy came from the woods." Duncan threw the papers across the room. "I don't care about any of this. You can't make me listen to you. It won't be long before things change around here. It won't be long. You've trapped me here. I'm not some item you can put on a shelf and expect to collect dust. Nope. So, why don't you teach yourself something?"

"You don't have to talk to me that way, Duncan. I'm not the enemy here. I'm trying to help you. I changed your diapers."

"If it wasn't for the man in my dreams, I wouldn't have known. I dream about him all the time. He told me I was not of this world. The folks in town know all this, too. Don't worry, Andrea. I'm not mad. I would've lied, too! No big deal."

He offered his mother a blank stare of confusion and pushed away from the table where educational papers covered Andrea's certification. Andrea felt her heart pounding from the pain in her head. "I've got a migraine. I'm going to lie down for a while."

Duncan found the pair of scissors in the bathroom. His parents were out like a light. Before entering his parents' bedroom, Duncan turned to look down the hallway. "I'm going to show her that I don't want to be home schooled.

She's not going to trap me here." He walked over to Andrea's sleeping body and Duncan began to cut her hair. Handfuls of dark hair covered the floor. In the darkness, a childish laughter echoed with the squeaking of a pair of corroded scissors. He left piles of hair along the carpet leading to his bedroom, a place he kept clean and organized. After placing his mother's hair throughout the house, he parted the curtains and stared out at the woods. The trees whispered to Duncan; distant voices calling out from beyond the branches of his home.

Someone stood in the dark. A tall, ominous shadow moved through twisted thickets and fallen limbs. Duncan followed the sound of the whispering trees. His feet took him to the end of the road. With his long, thin arms, he reached out and screamed. Lights turned on in distant windows. Neighbors from miles and miles up the road opened their doors and listened to the deafening cry of Duncan Langer. Charles and Andrea ran down the road to their son. His scream continued for several minutes. Duncan did not take one single breath as his mouth opened wider and wider, pulling his skin across his cheek bones, stretching his ears to the back of his head. Andrea pulled away from Duncan.

"Jesus Christ," Charles cried, holding Andrea in his arms. "He's calling out to him. The

Listener. We've got to leave. Pack our things and go."

Figures appeared in the distance, talking loudly, kicking rocks as their feet fumbled along the road. After nearly four minutes, Duncan stopped screaming. The unnerving silence fell across the hills, but the absence of Duncan's scream did not stop the large crowd in the darkness. Puffs of cigarette smoke rose from soft mumbles and chuckles. Andrea could not see their faces. Charles squinted and tried his best to make out the uninvited guests.

"Hold it right there," Charles said, holding his hand out as if he could force them back with his mind. "You have no right being here. Our son was sleep walking. That's all."

Andrea wept as Charles spoke. "We apologize for the noise. It's late. Let's all get back to sleep. What do you say?"

"I say we burn that little bastard alive," a deep voice said from the crowd. It was a man's voice. Charles could not identify the individual. "We don't know why you're all still here, locking yourselves up like crazed recluses. You come in and out of town when you please, ignoring our town hall meetings and you've never signed one of our petitions. Who the hell do you people think you are? You're not wanted here. You and your screwed-up kid. Do you know what they say about him in school? Do you? Even his teacher hates him. Kid can't learn. Doesn't want to get anything through his head."

"Get the hell off my property," Charles shouted. "Get the hell out of here. Now. Go! Go!"

Wordlessly, their neighbors turned around and vanished into the darkness. Andrea and Charles walked Duncan to the door where they paused. In the silence, Charles felt like a family, only for a moment. His grief somehow managed to sneak away into the night. He did not care what the neighbors thought or how Duncan's teacher felt about him. He just wanted Duncan to be normal. Charles remembered when he fell off his bike when he was five. He bled like everyone else. His scabbed knees were not different either.

Charles took his family into the living room. With large, frightened eyes, Charles pulled Andrea to him. "What happened to your hair? Christ, you've got bald spots everywhere. Jesus."

Andrea touched her head and screamed. She saw the piles of hair scattered throughout the hallway and living room. She glared at Duncan. "How could you do this? How could you?" By the time Charles was standing across the room, he heard the slap. Duncan fell to the floor. "You're not who I thought you were," she screamed. "You're a monster. You're crazy." With her hair in her hands, she ran up the stairs sobbing. While Andrea slept, Charles put their son to bed, the very son they had prayed for and wanted throughout the years. He no longer felt connected to his family; the world appeared to move away from him the closer his fingers came to scratching the surface of all he wanted to know. Who was Duncan Langer? Could the child summon The Listener back to their home? Will the neighbors contact the local authorities regarding Duncan's recent midnight screaming episode?

"Dad," Duncan whispered as Charles stood in the bedroom doorway. "Do you love me? I don't think you love me anymore?"

"Goodnight, Duncan."

"You didn't answer me."

"I'm tired of answering to you, Duncan. Do you know what you did to your mother? Do you? How about the incident tonight? Screaming like a crazy person? I don't know what to do with you. You've got to change. You have to."

"If I don't!"

"Goodnight, Duncan!"

The morning sun flooded the house. It was no longer a place to raise a child but a place to bury one. Andrea poured herself a cup of coffee, gathered dirty clothes from the floor, and skipped across the mirror so she would not see the frightful image of her hair, scraggly, bald, and worrisome. With one hand holding Duncan's dirty boxers, Andrea pulled the chain to the light in the basement. The old washing machine bounced up and down, vibrating the various bottles of detergents on the unleveled shelf. Andrea could feel a stranger's eyes staring at her from the shadows, lurking between the wooden beams, waiting to reach out and snatch her and pull her down into a darkness.

"Jesus, it's cold!" Andrea's breath filled the air. One would imagine her smoking in the basement. She rubbed her hands together. "Much better," she whispered. "Much better."

After she slammed the lid to the washing machine shut, she came face to face with her special gift, her midnight demon. Duncan's eyes were a maddening storm, filled with shadows, unwilling to catch the light squeaking in from the basement window. His arms were folded across his chest, lips quivering and forehead sweating. Andrea felt a great sense of pity for her son. But, as she watched him move from the stairs to the window, he began to laugh. No one told Duncan Langer a joke.

"You startled me," Andrea said, moving for the stairs. "I thought you were outside playing in the fields. I know we told you not to go outside. Do you know why we told you not to go outside? Do you?"

Duncan stood in silence.

"You can ignore me all day, Duncan. I don't care. You know what you did was wrong. How could you cut my hair off? I love my hair. You just cut it off. I can't show my face around here. People will laugh at me."

"That's what I want them to do. I want them to laugh at you. Soon enough, you'll know what it feels like to be me." Duncan's voice had finally reached the edge of puberty, sinking lower and lower in the webbed shadows of a darkened room. "I know I'm not of this world. I know the truth. I want to go back to where I came from. The man in the woods will come, mommy. He will and when he does I'm gonna jump in his arms and he'll carry me back home. I'd rather walk among the woods and fields than stay here in this house with you two miserable pieces of shit."

Andrea began to laugh. The sounds of her laughter aggravated Duncan. He clenched his fists. The truth had to be told. Andrea's smile disappeared. "You don't belong to the woods or the fields. You don't belong to this world. You're not from here. You're from the fiery pits of hell. That's where you'll go when this is all over."

"We'll see," Duncan grimaced.

Andrea climbed the stairs, leaving Duncan in the basement by himself. She would find a way to deal with Duncan. She had been afraid of him for years, searching the halls for his figure or cupping her ears to listen to the sounds of his footsteps. His face found its way into her dreams, and she knew in that particular moment what had to be done. She would see it through. She quickly slammed the basement door shut. She pulled three locks together and pushed against the door. Click.

She collapsed. Paint ships fell to the floor as Duncan's fists pounded against the weak wooden beams. Things would never be the same again. Andrea knew the unpleasant child behind the basement door would try to escape. Perhaps crawling through the small, square window in the corner of Duncan's new room would be his first idea. The cellar door would have to be boarded shut. As the evening sky grew dark behind the black, bent branches of the woods, Charles hammered the last rusty nail into a piece of wood. "That should do it," he coughed, inhaling the cold, burning air. "He'll never get out of here. I know I couldn't. What do you think of all my hard work, huh?" He lifted his hands over his head as if to display one's final masterpiece. Andrea smiled.

"I think it looks wonderful. You don't think the neighbors will hear him down there now do you? I mean, what if someone hears him? What'll we say?" Andrea's concerned eyes lowered to Charles as he placed his box of tools on the ground. He sighed.

"No one's gonna hear that little prick down there. Not a soul. Do you hear anything? All I hear is the wind."

Andrea listened as the branches in the distance twisted together, reaching for the purple horizon. The wind pushed through the trees as leaves danced through unpaved pathways. The golden hills vanished as the sun crawled beneath the tops of the skeletal tress. "I don't hear a thing. This'll work. We'll have to feed him you know?"

Charles nodded. He carried the tools to his shed in the back. He kept most things back there. Many of those things he never used unless he found work and had to go in to collect the necessary tools. As he slowly closed the door to the shed, he saw a shadow moving against the cracks in the small window beneath the house. Duncan must have started a small fire. Charles ran around the house to Andrea. "I think he's made a fire down there, Andrea! I mean, hell. What are we gonna do with this kid?"

"He won't burn the house down, Charles. He knows he'll die. He's got too much to lose here and I'm getting sleepy. What do you say we call it a day? I'm cold."

Charles threw his arm around his wife's shoulder, warm, comforted, and weary. They opened the basement door and placed a plate of food on the top step. Their eyes watched as

Duncan walked around a small fire he made. He placed his foot on the fire and stomped it out. "The light will have to do."

Disconnectedness had made its way into the hall where Charles and Andrea Langer stood. "You can close the door now. You don't have to stand up there staring at me. Goodnight."

Andrea kicked the basement door shut. They sat up in bed, listening to the sounds of Duncan kicking cans around in the basement. Andrea figured the nights were going to be the most difficult. Charles poured Andrea another glass of wine. It was bitter.

"My goodness," Andrea chuckled, wiping her lips with her wrist. "I don't know if I like it. How long do you think this is going to last? How long do we have to keep him down there? We locked up our own child."

"Enough wine for you," Charles said, removing the glass from her fingers. "You've got to understand what's going on here. Andrea, we were given a child and warned that if one of us were to expire, he'd turn into some devil. Well, Duncan has clearly transformed before his time." Charles grinned.

"There's nothing funny about it, Charles! Nothing."

"Look, I don't know how long he's gonna be down there because I don't know how the hell to get rid of the kid. What are we gonna do? Kill him? Bury him in the woods? I don't think so. We willingly took him, Andrea. Whoever or whatever came to our door that night knows what's going on here in this farmhouse. Why'd we move here, anyway? The farmhouse!"

"Shush it," Andrea demanded. "Do you know how long my grandfather worked on this place? How much money these walls swallowed?"

"Too bad they don't spit." Charles attempted to hold back his smile.

"I've always wanted to live here. You told me you loved the place. We've got to be the most stupid parents in the world."

"No way. That'd surprise me."

"I believe it's time for us to go into town and talk with someone. We can't live like this. I know you don't like the idea, Charles. I do. But, we're not going to keep him locked down there forever."

"Who should we talk to?"

"Reverend Walter Holloway. He's the guy who helped those people a few years ago, remember? He helped them with their child. It was deformed or something."

"I don't remember."

"Good. You'll sleep better than me tonight."

The old man could not walk like he used to; pulling himself along the cold, metal railing of the church offered him one way in and one way out. For being rather impersonal and menacing, he found gratitude in his heart for the people who lived in town. He owed everything to them. Or did he? He carefully lifted his legs to the final step, pushed opened the large, wooden door, and rubbed his nose. "Must've caught this somewhere on the East-side," he whispered, while walking through the narrow hallway. The church was dark. Perhaps a mouse scurried here and there, but nothing truly disturbed Reverend Holloway. Nothing. He lived in a tiny room above where the congregation sat every Sunday.

He was visibly disturbed on this still, autumn night, waiting for the townsfolk to come knocking on his door, shouting, screaming, crying; he felt different. They were a rather superstitious bunch; locked together in religious torment and fear. Fear changed everything for Holloway in those days as he finished his last cup of coffee and glared out of his study window. Books covered his desk. A sour, sweaty smell had taken over the room through the years. He knew how arduous it was living in an isolated town, a place where no one with a caring heart could hear a scream. This was the last place in the world to stop and visit; not the kind of town where a large family could park along the side of the road and snap pictures. This was the kind of town that would run a sorrowful soul out on a rail. No questions asked. That's the problem, Holloway thought, lighting a candle.

He'd been hiding for years now, avoiding the blank, frightful stares of the congregation. They were speaking about the Langer's son again. It didn't help that the last candle in the church blew out when one of the older women stood up and shouted at Holloway, demanding him to remove the child from the Langer's house, for his howling could be heard for miles and Old Scratch managed to slip through their fingers and come to town. Holloway calmed all their fears with words from the gospel and dismissed them, waving his hand in the air as if to send all dark energy to the wind. "Allow the wind to care for this matter," he shouted, caressing his long, white beard. "Be gone."

He'd known of the Langer's for a considerable amount of time. After Andrea Langer's grandfather passed away, she came sailing in with her new husband. I believe he's a handyman, Holloway thought. That's what he is.

He saw two figures moving in the night as small snowflakes landed on slated rooftops; he was no longer alone. Outside, the wind began to whistle through the tiny openings between the bricks of the church. There were times when Holloway thought he'd heard some unknown voice moving around in the dark, shuffling through his study and drifting along the steps outside. Things moved in the dark. Holloway knew better than anyone else in town; the sins of others always come out into the light. The darkness may hold them in silence, but truth demands to be heard. Holloway had no control over the power of darkness and light and the overpowering burdens Reverend Holloway carried because of these hapless souls made him feel older than he looked, much older.

A soft knock interrupted his thoughts as his eyes shifted to the house at the end of the street. The Langer house. Andrea Langer's grand-father, George Langer, never spoke to anyone. Hell, it was hard enough getting the mean-spirited bastard to attend church. He lived in the farmhouse until the day Hell opened its gates or Heaven, Holloway did not know. The Morning George passed away, Holloway secretly found a way into the Langer's home and forgave George for all his sins, sins no man knew, sins no man wanted to know. George's wife had died decades earlier. Perhaps George's own grief had killed him.

Reverend Holloway stared out at two familiar faces in the night. He could see Charles Langer holding his wife, Andrea. I was just thinking about these troubled souls, he thought and allowed them inside. Soundlessly, they made their way through the large room where worshippers fell on their knees and trailed along a narrow tunnel. Holloway did not know when the church had been erected.

In Reverend Holloway's study, Holloway sat with Charles and Andrea Langer as they cried. Their sobs could be heard echoing down the long, uninhabited corridors of the old church. As their harrowing cries died down, Holloway coughed. He yearned to hear any sound other than the suppressed emotions of the Langer family.

"I knew this time would come. It had to." Before Reverend Holloway removed his coat, Andrea's head fell back on the chair.

"We've exhausted all of our options, Reverend. I know I haven't been an outstanding citizen, but I don't know where else to go. We've thought about this for a longtime. We can't handle our son, Duncan. He's changed. When he was brought to us...I mean," Andrea paused. Charles looked furious. "When we had him, we knew something was wrong. He didn't fit in with other boys his age, almost distant and cruel for no apparent reason. We locked him in the basement, Reverend. We had to. Please, don't judge us. Are we going to hell? I know I'd send someone to hell for locking their child in the basement."

Andrea's attempt to fill the room with humor faded. Her eyes watched as Holloway opened a book with names scrawled across the pages. Charles leaned over Holloway's collection of theological books and squinted his eyes. "Those names," Charles said, frowning. "Where did those names come from? Who are those people?"

"These are children," Holloway answered, turning the pages of the book. "Children who now belong to the lost cities of the underworld. Here, we create sins. Never again shall I pass a sin to another. Never again." Reverend Holloway closed his eyes. No one knew what kind of horrors were spinning their webs behind his wrinkled face. When his eyes opened, Andrea and Charles held the book of names in their hands.

"Give that back," Holloway demanded. "Few eyes are allowed to read those names. For reasons beyond your own understanding, I've kept them safe for years. Most of the locals thought I burned it thirteen years ago. Well, after I relieved them of the last child. Read the name on the bottom."

As parents, they felt excited. As people, they felt sick. There, on the bottom of the page, written in black ink was the name Duncan Langer. Charles stood up. "What the hell is this? What is this shit?"

"Calm down, Mr. Langer. I'll explain everything to you. You've got to understand that I was left with no choice. I work for these people. They've fed me, clothed me, nurtured me, and I couldn't refuse them just as I can't refuse you.

Living one's life in such a manner can destroy the soul, working for two things. Two of everything. It's madness. Entire generations have passed through here, people with no name, clothes, or money. They longed for something more. Over the years, families became close. Quite close!"

Reverend Holloway walked gracefully to the window; he was a towering figure, almost saintly and authoritative. The stars illuminated his frame. With clasped hands and a saddened face, Holloway turned away from the window.

"As whole generations moved here, scrambling for scraps of food, digging ditches for a new life, interbreeding occurred. Violent molestations during those unpredictable times were not at all a rarity, for I've watched groups of children murdered because of their deformities. Oh, how their faces cried out in the night. They burned most of those children in the woods behind your home. It wasn't always a simple farmhouse. I knew your grandfather, George." The Reverend circled around his desk and set his hand on Andrea's shoulder. "He was, unquestionably, the most intelligent man in the region. Always keeping to himself. Fearful of the locals as he had been an outsider. He heard the stories; he simply didn't wish for them to be true."

"He spoke of screams from the woods," Andrea said. "I remember as a young girl, playing outside on the edge of the wheat field. There was a child crying. I ran into the farmhouse to tell pappy, but he didn't want to hear anything I had to say. I forgot. Goodness."

"When the second world war broke out, people were terrified of everything. They were staring into the trees, waiting for a communist to come falling down. The level of fear in those days was deeply uncomfortable. So, as these families breed, I give their children away. I'm the man who visited you that October night. It's somewhat surprising how far a robe and a jar of mud will go. I knew you wanted a child. So, I gave you one."

Charles and Andrea could not believe what they were hearing from the tired old man with the long, white beard. Could he be trusted, Charles thought?

"It was you," Andrea whispered. "You came to our home, promised us a child and he turns out to be the son of one of these inbred hillbillies? You've got to be kidding me. Charles, do you have anything to say to this man?"

Charles felt the tremors in his hand. The sharp pain crawled up his left shoulder and fell down to his wrist. "Shit," Charles said. "My whole arm's gone numb."

"Anxiety," Reverend Holloway said. "If I were to receive such news, I'd probably die. My years have come to an end here in this little town. They'll find another. He'll perform my duties. Protect the secrets of this place as all the others had done before. Cultivate lies to win over the bleeding hearts of young couples. Time repeats itself. It does. But, repetition is hell. Who wants to live in hell for the rest of their lives? I know I don't."

Everything Charles fought for in his life came rushing back to his mind, waves of stories and disappointments and failed dreams. All of it had come together in a rather peculiar way; the truth forced all of those things to form in his mind as Charles lifted his wife from a chair. They were filled with terror, an icy, surreal terror like the haunting drumming of a quickened pulse. Andrea's tears soaked her blouse.

"Please, do not run in fear. Fear creates things here in this town, a town of secrets. Have I not given you all the answers? Have I not told you about the murders behind your home and all the evil things I had to do? They would've killed me if I told anyone. If they found out you two came here, into their place of worship, they'd kill me. I don't know how they'd kill me, but they most certainly would. They threatened me before, I'm sure they'll threaten me again. You've got to kill him! Do you understand?

There's no way out of this horrifying mess. I helped create all this. I did."

Charles forced a smile. "We'll be gone in the morning. I'll gather our things and head out first thing. There's a chance for us, right?"

"I'd like to believe there's a chance for us all in this crazed world," Reverend Holloway said. "I've become weak living here, feeding their horrors and sins daily, consoling their losses as another child is born with crooked teeth and bulging eyes filled with blood."

"Duncan's a cute kid. I don't see how he came from an incestuous family. There were moments when I thought he looked like me. I forced myself to believe it. He looked like his old man."

"Many of these children are not just weighed down by physical abnormalities, Charles Langer. How nice it was for you to take your wife's last name. Such an unconventional thing to do, I imagine."

"What the hell are you saying?"

"Most of those children who had been burned alive behind your home in those woods were not three-eyed beasts with hooves, Mr. Langer. Most of them displayed profoundly unusual behavior. As the child grows, the child remains silent, obedient and vigilant. When puberty hits, the child is capable of killing. I couldn't kill your son. I've never killed a single human being while serving this ghastly well of nightmares and sin.

I promised myself I'd leave after I told you all of this. I guess I will. I don't know."

"Don't you think it's in your best interest to get the hell out of here while you still have a chance?" Langer asked. "They'll come for you in the morning when they see our car gone. You know it."

"I'll make up my mind by dawn. Now, you must go! Take care of that child! Make him disappear! Find a way! There's a couple on the other side of town who gave birth to a baby girl a few days ago. The first child to be born here in thirteen long years. The town would like me to go see about it. Another one. I don't know what I'll do with this poor soul."

"Another reason to leave, Reverend Holloway. You don't have to die here. You can leave with us. We'll take you with us."

"No. Out of the question. I'll find my own way, Mr. Langer. Thank you for being so kind. Do you forgive me?"

"We'll see," the Reverand said. "We'll see."

Charles and Andrea entered the house without a sound. They listened for Duncan. Nothing. Charles instructed Andrea to place all of her clothes in the purple suitcases he'd recovered from a yard sale before he decided to jump in bed with Andrea Lee Langer. They tossed clothes throughout the room, often pausing to wait for the sounds of Duncan's voice rising up from the wooden boards. Nothing. They continued collecting personal items during the night, gazing out windows as they carried small suitcases to the door, waiting for a figure in the window, waiting for a knock on the door, waiting for a voice to stir outside, waiting for the town to come and kill them all, waiting for all things dark and maddening.

The Langer's placed all of their essentials in suitcases near the front door; they were ready for anything. Having a gun would certainly provide their grim situation with some comfort, but Charles refused to file for one. Time slipped away. Both Charles and Andrea held each other as they waited for the night to welcome the day.

"Did we get everything? Andrea asked. "I don't want to leave anything behind. Especially the things my mother had given me before I moved up here. I remember her telling me how much I'd adore the scenery. Imagine that! The scenery! I wonder if she ever thought I'd enjoy the company of the locals. Vicious, psychotic animals. I recall you bringing up a conversation related to a cellphone. Remember? That would've helped. Never did file for a gun."

"Shut up," Charles cried, jumping to his feet. He looked out the door. Tall shadows surrounded the mailbox. The quiet confused

Charles. "They're out there. Stay down. I'm going to the basement. Keep the door locked. They can't get in."

Charles checked all the locks on the basement door. "Good," he said. "Safe and sound." He hurried down the hall and stopped before the entrance to the back porch. Things moved out there he could not quite understand. "Jesus Christ!"

"They've surrounded the entire place," Andrea whispered, crawling on her hands and knees across the floor. They held each other as they pressed their bodies on the basement door, waiting for Duncan to punch threw the wood, snarling, screaming. Voices whispered and died out as the sun filled the kitchen windows. Sleep had caught them. When Charles finally realized he'd fallen asleep, he nudged Andrea. "Get up," he said. "Sun's up. I'm gonna look out the window."

As his eyes peered over the sink, the golden fields and bright horizon filled his heart with an unexpected joyfulness he hadn't felt in years. He wanted to leave the Langer farmhouse; he never wanted to leave New York City for some isolated town filled with abandonment and mystery. "Enough is enough," Charles said, searching the cabinets for nonperishables. "Honey, is there anything in here you'd like me to grab? Andrea,

I think we've got more of that stuff you like in the other pantry down the hall."

Andrea followed her husband's shadow as it made its way across the horrendous floral wallpaper in the kitchen. He screamed. When his body hit the floor, Andrea thought Duncan had opened the basement door. "Charles? Are you okay? Charles?" Andrea stood up and walked into the kitchen where she found her husband shaking violently. His fingers curled as his teeth pierced through his bottom lip. Droplets of blood stained his shirt. Andrea knew what was happening, she felt it in her soul, that seemingly forbidden place where emotions are allowed to pull everything apart. Charles was having a heart attack. She lifted his head and stared into his eyes, smiling. He coughed.

"You have to get out of here," he gurgled, holding his chest. "Get the suitcases and get to the car. Don't sit here with me."

"I can't leave you here, Charles. I can't do it. I'm going to carry you to the porch. I'll pull the car around and we're gone. Do you hear me, Charles?"

Charles stopped breathing. Although most of their years had been spent living in silence and grief, Andrea realized for the first time how much she loved the man lying on the floor, the same man who packed up everything he owned and drove her across the country, seeking new adventures away from the bustling life of the city. She wept. Her tears streamed down her pale face, saturating her husband's shirt. She thought about falling asleep on his chest, waiting for the basement door to open. Duncan would come out, smile at the horrific scene, and murder her while she slept. She wanted Duncan to do just that. Unfortunately, Andrea Langer could not muster the courage to follow her own plans; she had to listen to Charles, and leave.

The front door opened. The quietness of the countryside allowed her to hear nearly every bird and fallen leaf. Nothing. She ran around to the back of the house where the car was parked. After fumbling for her keys, she managed to open the driver's side door and jump in. Leaving the suitcases behind did not bother her so much. The man lying dead on the floor in the kitchen bothered her. As she turned the ignition, expecting to hear the explosive sound of the car's engine, Andrea noticed that the cellar door had been crushed in. Piles of wood surrounded discarded cans of beer and spray-paint; she'd never been good at keeping up with the yard.

The car did not start. An ear-splitting screech filled her head. "No, no, no!" A chill touched the surface of her flesh, a memory of something she'd lost a long time ago came back to her. She jumped out of the car and moved her feet along the cut path to the front door. She no longer cared about Duncan. The town did not frighten her anymore. Death created her own strength. She pulled the locks from the basement door, threw it open and stared down at the bottom of the dimly lit stairs.

"Come on out," she screamed, placing her feet on the top step. "Come on out and play, Duncan. Don't you want to play with me?" She pulled a sharp kitchen knife from her waist, anxious and shaking as hurried feet approached her from behind. She felt tiny hands push against her back and the ceiling and the stairs twirled around and around in her eyes. She landed on the cold, basement floor. She could not move. As she gently moved her wrist, a tiny, white bone punctured her skin. "Jesus," she said, rolling on her back. "Shit!"

Duncan stood at the top of the stairs; his dark eyes appeared to be searching the walls. As Andrea's bruised body rested on the cold basement floor, she watched as Duncan bound her hands, cautiously looking up and down at his mother's face. "This should do for now. In the meantime, I suggest you get some rest. I'm going to take dad out back. You don't mind. I know you don't."

A yellow gelatin formed across her left eye, causing tremendous discomfort and blindness. The swelling heated her entire face, a sharp burning pain ran down her side to her lower thigh where shards of glass stuck to her flesh. Pulling against the water pipe was pointless. She knew he'd come down later and end it all. She felt it. Duncan tugged on his father's arms, sliding his spine across the wooden floorboards. Outside, he placed Charles' body near the cellar door. The others had come. Faceless strangers surrounded the farmhouse. Many of them appeared to be lost. Pale faces glared at Duncan as he wiped sweat from his forehead.

"One moment," Duncan said, walking through the cellar door.

Andrea forcefully shook her head as she saw her son standing over her with a knife. He waved it around as if he was going to play with her, cut her up slowly like a toy doll. "Did you drop something?" Duncan asked, placing the end of his finger on the knife's razor edge. "That was quite the tumble. Thought you'd use this? I don't think so." As the silver blade touched Andrea's throat, she swallowed. Tears fell between the cracks of her lips. "Duncan, please. I'd never hurt you. I'm sorry I didn't listen to you. Mommy is so sorry. I could've done better."

"This situation has become unpleasant," Duncan said. "I guess you couldn't handle me. Now, I guess I have to go someplace else. I loved you. Come on in guys. Take her."

Duncan pulled the knife away. A group of featureless shadows pulled her by the arms to the cellar door. Andrea closed her eyes and waited in the darkness for an end. She could hear the townsfolk talking amongst themselves. They carried Andrea Lee Langer into the field; both feet and hands were held by unsteady hands. Men, women, and children laughed as she was thrown to the ground. The smell of burning flesh filled the air. She saw her husband, Charles, wrapped in flames. Flesh melted from his face, exposing the whiteness of his skull. As Andrea watched her husband's burning corpse, she saw a man standing next to her. A recognizable face looked down at her.

"I told you to leave, Andrea. You didn't listen. I listen, you see. I've always listened. You waited too long. I don't know if I'm sorry."

Reverend Holloway motioned for the others with a simple gesture of the hand. Her saddened face gazed out at the old farmhouse for one last time.

"This is a sad day for us all," Holloway shouted to the townsfolk. "We haven't had a burning here in many years. Now, Andrea Lee Langer must follow the smoke of all those who have come before her. Even in death we find fear. Life is not easy. So, I must confess my sorrow for this poor soul. Burn her!"

The flames consumed her body in the middle of the field. The gathering of people slowly moved through the golden pasture of death, leaving two bodies burning; ashes danced with the wind as Reverend Holloway took Duncan's hand.

"Now, we're going to have to find you a new home," Reverend Holloway said. "What do you think about that? A whole new family? No more yelling, screaming, fighting? It's all over now, Duncan Langer. Come. We'll find you a new family."

"Sounds wonderful."

The Daemonum
Signature

I felt shame as I rested my head against the window, gazing out at a blanket of white outside the stone walkway of St. Augustine Monastery. Should I believe in the power of God? Often times I feel as if we all have gathered beneath the shadows of our past here. We bury ourselves deep in the ground and occasionally above it, where the images of our Lord can be seen crucified above every entrance, a face of death and horror has become more of a friend to my isolation than the scriptures I diligently memorize, a peculiar comfort in the eyes of loss. Although I have never quite endured such pain in my life, I can only imagine how tumultuous and frightening our Lord's life had been. Whispers of old age, dying faith, and a crumbling monastery rose from darkened rooms of fellow believers. These men were the kind of religious fundamentalists who, without silhouetted faces of doubt, wandered the woods together, pondering the old ways and the new ways, a glorifying release from the beastly odor of sin, murder, adultery, and fear.

The shame became connected to the life I had been living, a life born in the dismal streets of an unimpressive town along the Mississippi. I have always been ashamed of my loyalty to God. My own memories of childhood were shrouded in beatings, sleepless nights, and a lovely game of hide and seek. My father would stumble through the house, knocking over cans and chairs, waking up the block. Mother would hide. We'd all hide. We had no choice. We were a Catholic family, born and raised in the light of Christ. One could not and would not argue the concept of religion with my parents as they were devout and strict. My sister ran away from home shortly after my fifteenth birthday. I never saw her again.

I decided to join St. Augustine after my studies were completed years later. I discovered much in Rome as I sat with many young men who had been misguided; they lost their way and found the eyes of Christ calling out to them. These people were not my friends. In fact, I believe it's safe to say I never had many friends. Monsignor Francis once labeled me as being "incompetent" and "immoveable." I never gave much thought to these judgments as I found Francis to be arrogant, uncouth, and deceptive. On a still night, when fat snowflakes skipped across slatted rooftops, shame fell over me and the images of those men wrapped together, flesh with flesh, forced me to consume the remaining communion wine. Shame.

Silence is one of those things that can lift a man's soul or destroy it. I'm not quite certain which one of those adventures I'll take but observing Monsignor Francis engaging in abnormal behavior with younger men behind the Parish gardens haunted me. Their twisted faces, calling out in joy and muffled sin, crawled through me like an infection, poisoning me, almost draining my body of its courage to find some answer to what I had seen hours before. How many were there, anyway? Could my own damaged mind remember their boyish faces, those tormented souls manipulated by the higher forces of our church, utilizing guilt as a weapon against our youth in the midst of both their confusion and denial? I could never admit such horrors out loud, for I must, as all those with secrets must do, write my thoughts down with the assistance of ink, paper, and wine.

My youthfulness has faded. I can see my aged reflection through the cold glass of winter, a hapless smirk or a threadbare coat had been the only redeeming attributes to my own character throughout the years. Oh, how things demand to be felt and changed. They must.

The snow outside the window slowly disappeared into darkness. A knock on the door pulled me from my reflective state.

"Come," I shouted, pulling away from the desk near the window. The room appeared to be lifeless, the walls unadorned, the moaning floorboards with weak ceiling tiles. I had always felt like a prisoner at St. Augustine.

"Father Fairview?" a voice whispered. "May I speak with you for a moment? There's something you should know."

I gestured for Brother David to move into the light. I kept a candle burning day and night. The power had been restored at St. Augustine over a decade ago.

"What is on your mind?" I asked.

He revealed a face of concern, as if there had been a fire burning in the hallway and he could not muster the strength to convey the news of such a monstrous catastrophe.

"I have been working on a few cases in the local area," David explained as he sat down in a chair in the corner of the room. "Such tasks we have, Fairview. I am essentially concerned about Francis. He hasn't been himself. Because of these cases and the monsignor's impersonal behavior, I feel lost. I've prayed about it."

"Prayer can only do so much," I said. "We learn to live with the duty God brings forth. Although such duties may be left to be attended to by the others in our church, your duty belongs to God. Share his words."

His face turned into a ferocious dog. He placed a brown folder in my hands and, again, sat down to release a sigh. "There's a girl across the river. She seems to be causing an unusual disturbance in her house. Objects moving by themselves, voices, unexplained noises in the night. You know how these things go. One moment you're waiting to see Rome and the next, you're staring the Devil in the eyes. This one is different."

"David, I've been a priest for decades. I've seen so much of this wonderful world. However, I have also seen it's cruelty, it's meaninglessness. But, we have to ignore that which consumes us. Fear. Fear can be exercised by the power of prayer. Lord knows, I've been working tirelessly to find a solution to St. Augustine's issues. We need new pipes in the basement. The water heater is currently knock-ing on death's door and we haven't seen one penny from the Vatican."

"Damn the Vatican," he shouted, lifting his body from the chair. "I didn't seek you out to be patronized. I don't care about the integrity of St. Augustine's structure and anatomy. There's a

116

family that requires our immediate assistance. This young girl I speak of has a gift. Fairview, I do not believe she belongs to Lucifer. She has a map."

"A map?"

"Correct. A map."

"To what?"

"The map is inside her head. She knows where it's located. The very item we've been searching for, Fairview. This could help us get out of here. We could finally overpower Francis and perhaps rebuild St. Augustine to its former richness."

"You have to be out of your mind, David. Do you know what you're talking about? Going behind Francis and using some innocent girl to locate this legend! It's a myth, David. It's all a lie. There never was a key. Never will be. Hell exists right here." I stood up and placed my finger on his forehead, but he recoiled. Fear has its own agenda. I knew of the key. The Lost Key of Eternity. It had been rumored for centuries that the key had fallen into the hands of Hitler's regime. Everyone sought it. Most died because of it. I knew it was real.

"Believe me Brother David when I tell you that such a key is a myth. And you have been bewitched by some girl who probably cannot read a single verse from the Old Testament.

Goodness, I've grown weary for the night. I'm tired."

Brother David sat in my chair as if it were going to be the last chair he'd enjoy. Built by the eloquent craftsmanship of the French, I pulled such a chair across Europe and thirty-nine states.

"We have an obligation to find this key. You must come with me tomorrow to speak with the girl. Her parents are deeply troubled. As I have noted before, Lucifer has his eyes on her. She's young, weak, and open to all dark forces in this world. I shall not allow it. No."

Quietness settled throughout the room. Shadows danced along the courtyard and stone walkway.

"We must leave early," I said. "We cannot allow Francis to know what we're doing. If any questions are asked, we are blessing the houses across the river. If what you say is true, we're looking at another war. Not the kind of war with guns and bombs. This could be the kind of war that allows whatever God sent down to Hell to come out. The key is just another tale to keep the young boys awake at night. Tomorrow it is. Do not fool me, Brother David."

"I'm not fooling you. I assure you, Fairview. What I have shared with you is unquestionably true. I shall not utter a single word. Tomorrow it is. Thank you, Father. Thank you."

I watched David leave the room, consumed by fear and concern. Because of his honesty and youthfulness, I could not ignore the issue at hand. The key. The key. Goodness, I thought, it would be David, right? He would be the one to locate it. While locking the brown folder in my desk, I heard scratching at the window. I blew out the candle. Such occurrences will grow, I thought. They always do.

The frozen trees were bleak skeletons resting against a landscape of ice and desolation. I greeted Brother David outside near the fountain. Such a special place for the soul to rest; I remember the vacant stare of the statue as I placed my hand on David's shoulder, pulling him closer to me. The sun pushed through the dismal clouds, creating shadows through the twisted branches of St. Augustine. David's eyes fought against my own. A different kind of sadness had fallen over his spirit, for David, as he most often did, caressed the fountain and pressed his fingers against the ice.

"There's an appealing strangeness about winter. It's so cold, hopeless. Then, you can see the beauty through the ice. I've learned to cherish the bitterness of nature."

David's voice cracked as he pulled away from the fountain. I placed the brown folder in his hands, expecting him to understand my anxiety, to see how painful it had been for me to turn those pages.

"You've read all the reports," he said, sitting down. I could relax.

I had read the reports collected by Brother David. I failed to realize how dedicated Brother David was to God. The truth spilled from those horrendous reports, outlining hundreds of bizarre events related to children being visited by apparitions and nightmares concerning a key. I felt the overwhelming fear of being seen; eyes could be watching.

"You must understand how imperative it is that you keep these reports locked away. If someone were to find those, we'd all be sent away to some pit in the middle of God knows where. Now, we must go. My knees hurt."

"You complain too much."

"Well, you must understand how time has crippled my body. Do not worry; it'll get to you as well. Now, I am deeply familiar with the inner workings of the occult as well as exorcism."

David elevated his head to glare over my shoulders. His eyes carried a familiar ache, a weeping child, afraid and alone. We walked through the woods where the river reached out into the trees. Moss drifted through the branches like curtains, flowing quietly against the wind, a soulful observation of such a scene cannot be captured in words. Frankly, I found myself captivated by the layers of ice confined below dead logs. David pointed across the river.

"There," he said, kicking the ground. "With keen eyes, one can see a row of small houses. Do you see them?"

"Yes."

Rage filled my heart as I placed my feet on the ice, testing my faith as I weighed my soul against God's will. I did not wish to cross the river, but I did not wish to leave Brother David alone. Ice cracked beneath our feet as we crossed the unmerciful countryside. "God would never allow us to fall," he said. "God is with us."

Goodness, I thought. The poor boy has lost it. How could he carry such a burden alone, a weighty anchor around his neck, bleeding his imagination and curiosity dry?

"We're not far now."

"Shut up," I screamed. "Carry on."

I entered a small room where a girl rested on a bed. Alongside an aged coffee table, I noticed a silver bowl filled with what looked like blood. An elderly gentleman leaned in the shadows, searching the room with his drunken eyes, shaking, waiting, and hurting. A large woman carried a glass of water to the seemingly reckless soul in the corner of the room.

Brother David spoke to the old man and woman quietly. How could such a soul be so compassionate and loving in the face of death?

The girl lifted her head, exposing the yellow-and azure-colored bruises along her pale flesh. Coldness filled the room. The girl's eyes opened; a clear emerald shine masked the horror behind her pupils. Death was in the room.

"David, would you kindly ask the mother to leave the room? This isn't going to be pleasant. I'll need you to keep the father in here. If she demands more strength, we'll have to allow this spirit to take over. That's not going to happen."

"You did read the reports. I informed you of the dangers, Father. I told you about the madness."

"If you do not remove that woman from the room, I'm going to have you placed before Monsignor Francis. I do not have time to argue about this girl's life. Now, go! Go!"

David followed my instructions accurately. The girl smiled at me. It had been one of those smiles that laughed at you. Yes, a smile. A smile can laugh. Its own quietness has a voice of thunder. Her frail arms, bent and curled around a frayed blanket, reached up into the air as if she were leaving the bed. A moan escaped from her lips. Madness, I thought. Yes, this is madness as it demands to be seen. The girl spoke to me. Her voice cut through me; a sharpened blade cursing the bones in my body and mocking my sight and restlessness.

"You're standing there thinking, 'Does God really give a fuck about me or have I simply wasted my life?' You're no man. You're no fucking man. You're a cunt. Well, I'd know. You never were a man. Hell, your sister ran away because she was smart. What'd you do? Run off to some cave and hide from the world because it was just too loud for you? You faggot. Cocksucker. Whore. Fuck you. Fuck you. Fuck you. Give it to me again, Daddy. Come on. Where's my father? Do you know he used to fuck me when mother attended her book club? Oh, how I enjoyed the sensation of being a woman, a free woman, freed by your father and released to the world as a whore."

"Silence," I shouted, removing my scarf. "You don't know who I am nor do you know why I am here. Who are you?"

"Don't ask," David said, returning from the hallway. "The mother is downstairs. If you ask her questions, she'll grow. It appears as if her soul relies upon our suspicions."

David swayed through the shadows of the room, hands folded behind his jacket.

"I am no demon!" shouted the girl. "I'm one of the ancients. One day, all the children of the world will have the key and enter through the doorway. All of those who have fallen have returned."

Such words forced me to retreat from the bedside. The air itself could only satisfy the decayed corpses of Hell.

"I suspect you have fallen. There's no need to highlight the past. Why do you occupy a child?" David spoke strongly.

"Children are easy. They pretend to fly. They live in a world adults loathe. We jump inside their bodies and we feel their passions and we enjoy it. The key has resurfaced. I know you're wondering why a young girl from the delta knows." Her laughter shook the wooden walls of the room. David gripped his chest.

"Liar," he whispered. "Liar. Liar. Liar. How dare you summon us and entertain us with your wicked lies. The key is gone. It's been gone for thousands of years. You walk among us, waiting to give it to a soul whose mind is filled with rocks and dust. Where's the key?"

"If your God had any idea," the girl laughed. "If he had any idea at all, he'd peel the skin from your bone and roast you over an open fire. He's good at that. Your God loves to roast his creations."

"Do not speak to me of my God. I demand you tell us where the key can be found."

"Who else knows about the possessions, David? Did you tell that little prick Fairview about Francis? Francis." She pushed the name from her lips. "He took you down into the chambers. Poor David, your sorrowful face and youthful charm never helped much. But, when he took off your pants and inspected your cock, you just couldn't get hard. Nope. You couldn't get hard because you know the truth. You're the only one. I am growing weak. There are fallen ones who walk in shame. Fairview knows a great deal about shame, correct? Oh, I know he does! I know he does! He feels it all the time. I wonder why you haven't sucked off your companion, David. I guess older men do not appeal to you."

"You blinded fiend. You cannot occupy this girl's body. You must leave it. It does not belong to you as you do not belong to this world or its beauty. What do you have for me, demon?"

"I have a map inside of my brain. There's a tomb on the outside of town. There's a large tree. Lightning strikes it once a year. Beneath those old stones, inside the tomb, you'll find the key. Hide it. Keep it hidden in the shadows. There are others jumping in and out of children. We're almost done. Finish the task. Find the key. Do you know what it unlocks, Brother David?"

Tears rolled down Brother David's face. Against the wall, where the shadows rolled down to the floor, I walked over to the girl's father.

"This demon is weak," I told him. "It's dying inside her. Don't worry about this. I must ask you to keep this between us. Your wife must never speak of this to anyone. Understood?"

The old man nodded and left the room.

"Tell us what it unlocks before you return to your home," I said, wiping David's tears with my scarf. "Questions give you power, but you shall be released once my question has been answered."

The girl looked into my eyes and laughed. "Father Fairview! Now, here's a man with grit. It unlocks the very place you people fear. It's the house of memory. Hell."

"The key unlocks the gates of Hell?" David's weakness ignited a spark of joy within the girl's eyes.

"Off to hell," she said. It had been done. The thing was no more.

We walked among the old houses, screams echoed against a darkening sky. Children wept as we passed. Hurried feet splashed through the mud. David walked a few feet behind me, opening his eyes and ears to the chaos of demons. I never fully believed in demons until I found David. After wandering through the woods for several hours, we rested near a crumbling wall. David spoke to me about the key and some mysterious gateway to a darker world. I will never quite understand why I journeyed with him to discover such an item.

David reached the top of the hill before I could. It had been his spiritedness, or perhaps his yearning for something more than what he had in his life that took him there. Routine.

"If we dare to rest now, the cold will gather around us and we'll be frozen. Let's go inside."

We entered a darkened hole, filled with rocks, sticks, and mud. The air, tainted with blood and decay, haunts my memory. Crawling through the darkness allowed all of my own profound insecurities to raise David's concern. My hands had been growing weak. My legs, bent and filled with fire, continued to pull my torso along the track of death. I saw a bright light. The orange glow filled up a larger room beneath the hill. As we entered the room, I noticed the walls and how they were constructed from limestone. A black box sat at the center of the room. David dropped to his knees and opened the box.

I cannot describe the precious item without walking through the pages of history, for the wind could never sing the item's song or compare its golden beauty to the Egyptians. The key was quite long, adorned with golden lilies and the faces of three young children.

"This key was held by King Solomon," David said, kissing the key, trembling with sweat and joy. "Throughout the ages, wars erupted and destroyed the lives of millions, sending a warning to the fallen who do not answer to God or Lucifer. These fiends are weary of our world. They want the door opened. They want back in."

"There are doors that cannot be shut once they're opened," I said. "The faces of those children show us that these vile creatures feast upon children and their weaknesses. Where's the door?"

"You're impatience irritates me!" David shouted, jumping to his feet. "I have the key. I know where the door is. Come. You must come with me."

"I've traveled enough. We have to talk about this, Brother David. We cannot open something that's unknown to us all. You're blinded by simple human curiosity."

In a moment, one can feel the universe throwing stones against one's chest. I demanded to know about Brother David's unsavory relationship with Monsignor Francis, but David's words faded as the cold wind blew through the hills. He held the key as if he were carrying an infant, a newly born beauty of the world. We slipped quietly through the back doors of St. Augustine. David turned around to depart; weakened by greed and power.

"Brother David?" One could recognize such a voice with a difficult memory. Francis stood before us, towering and enraged. He lifted his arm and pressed his index finger to his lips.

"Not a word," he said. "I have been looking all over these grounds for you frozen souls. Come, we must warm both of your cold bones."

We walked together in silence, passing darkened rooms, and turning down unending hallways.

"I suspect, Father Fairview has been observing your success here at St. Augustine, David. You've shown extraordinary promise. I've assured the others of your voracious yearning for knowledge as well as for things you should never know about."

I stopped. He knows about the key, I thought.

The priests were gathered together in shades of dancing light. Faces of hollowed apprehension and envy filled their eyes. The large room appeared to open up into a circular alter positioned on a slab of stone. When the door slammed shut, fearing both the alter and the anger in the room, I turned to leave.

"You're not going anywhere. In fact, you're never leaving St. Augustine again. Go!" Francis pushed me against David.

"Don't do this," I said. "You're asking far more than you can imagine."

"Give me the key!" Francis demanded.

The walls began to move as if water were running down from the ceiling. Voices blinded my vision. David dropped the key in Francis' hand.

"Take the world," David said. "It will never be the same again."

"We're opening the door so the spirits of evil can leave. Do you seriously believe they desire to stay here in this world of lifelessness, this cage of dust and rust? No. I think not."

The entire world passed away for a moment. Its death seemed almost quick, beating like that of a bat's wings, flapping in the night. All the demons of the world, the wandering skeletons of the night entered St. Augustine. The floor beneath me shook. Screams, cries, moans and curses filled my ears. The last breath of life had been taken from me as I watched endless white clouds of spirits circle the room. A vast space between our flesh and the icy chill within these horrid monsters crushed me. All the shame I felt, the indignity, the lust came flashing over me.

"And so the world shall be empty, a vacant space with no evil." Francis lifted his arms in the air as the other priests joined him.

David looked into Francis' eyes. "You fool," he said. "They're not leaving, they're coming through."

The Blues Singer of Crimson Parish

D aniel wanted to find a way to keep his secret safe. No one knew. How could they? It was locked away in a box upstairs, sleeping with the spiders and dust. There were secrets joined together with an ancient southern mystery whispering to the moon when he slept. Memories walked with the dead, evocatively following the murmurs of Daniel's heartache. He liked that. People stared at him. In a small town like Claiborne, wandering eyes, rumors, and unchanged generations of inquiring minds were the last thing on a young teenager's mind. "Let them stare," he would often whisper as he unloaded comic books from his threadbare shoulder bag.

Nirvana. "Let them stare all day long if they want to."

In Claiborne, people had a way of making a kid feel small, smaller than a kid should ever feel. When he arrived in Claiborne two weeks ago, after an unfortunate romance with his best friend, Harrison, who lived in a different Parish, Daniel felt compelled to run away, to cast his homework papers into the swamp, burn his journals, and follow the old dusty road to visit The Blues Man. Daniel Patterson moved away from home because his mother wanted him to have a more promising future. The drugs had never been an issue and his academic performance had never been condemned by his parents. The only issue had been Daniel's relationship with Harrison.

Harrison had lived down the street; occupied a dilapidated shack filled with a few dogs, one chicken, and a drunken father who chased his own dreams in the fields across from the swamps. Daniel never questioned Harrison about his mother. Harrison and Daniel had been best friends since Elementary school. They did everything together. They watched the trees disappear in the darkness of the sun's passing, cheerfully wandered the fields when there were more stars in the sky than anywhere else in Crimson Parish. They held hands when the birds broke apart and scattered away into the purple sky.

Daniel's departure changed everything. "We're leaving!" Daniel said. He cracked open a can of soda. He guzzled it down in a few minutes. Crushing the can with his right hand, he frowned and tossed the can into the trash bag along the back porch. His father had been collecting the cans for his new pair of glasses. Daniel's father collected more pennies than anyone else in the Parish. "I don't want to go. You know that." Daniel watched as Harrison smiled. He had one of those smiles that could imprison the heart of any girl in the state of Louisiana. Tall, slender, and handsome, Harrison had been one of the few guys Daniel had known who could walk through a mob of beautiful ladies without an upward glance. His disinterested face, along with his awful posture, indicated that Harrison was more in love with himself than with any girl in Louisiana. He was not interested in girls. "You're going where?" Harrison asked, closing his eyes. "I want to know?"

"I can't tell you."

"Why?"

"They don't want you to know."

"Right," Harrison sighed. "They're trying to protect you from being gay. That makes sense. What are they going to do, Daniel, throw you into one of those outback Nazi gay camps? Convert you?"

"No, of course not. But I want you to know that we're going to visit him."

"When?"

Daniel moved across the room slowly. His parents had left hours before. Daniel enjoyed Harrison more than he enjoyed himself. Perhaps Daniel felt as if the best part of his own personality came from Harrison, who always dared to ignite a fire of passion for life for Daniel in ways Daniel's parents could never possibly imagine. "After we're settled in," Daniel whispered, breathing against Harrison's sun-burned neck. Harrison's faded jeans and frayed T-shirt had seen more sweat and hard work than most of the good old boys down in New Orleans working on the barges. Harrison would often travel with his cousins to work on farms on the outskirts of town. Daniel could not find delight or satisfaction in working in the thickness of Louisiana's unbearable heat. He was an overconfident geek.

"So, we got caught. What's the big deal, Daniel? I mean, hell, people get caught giving blow jobs all the time. We can fight them, Daniel." Daniel could feel the confusion and grief in his eyes, Mississippi mud, almost dead, but still alive. He had the brownest eyes in the South.

"You're not even allowed in the house. If they knew you were here." Daniel paused, opened the window to look for his father's truck and turned away. "I'd probably never see or hear from you again."

"That's what they want."

Daniel and Harrison walked out to the lake where Daniel had lost his virginity to the boy standing beside him. Harrison Steele. "I'll come back," Daniel said.

"Promise."

"Promise."

Daniel watched the weeks slip off into silence and depression. The loneliness in Claiborne had broken him. His parents continued to move boxes into the rooms, decorate walls, and chat with the new neighbors while Daniel stared out the window, wishing for Harrison to crawl out from the darkness and take him back to the lake. "This is screwed up," he mumbled to himself as a fly slapped against his bedroom window. He did not like the new house. It smelled like plastic and fresh paint. That was enough for Daniel. He had decided long ago that he could never live a life worth living while sharing a house with his folks. "The Blues Man," Daniel whispered as he climbed the attic stairs. "He'll know what to do."

He opened a small, wooden box and removed a stained piece of yellow paper. "He lives at the end of Whitman Lane. You can hear his guitar through the trees. No one knows his name. We all call him, The Blues Man. You can ask him for anything. Be careful. Good luck. Lucile Hawkins. December 1927." The haunted Southern wind had given Daniel and Harrison the paper the night Harrison had unzipped his pants for the first time. Daniel had never ejaculated so quickly in his entire life. Daniel, feeling the oppressive heat through the wooden beams of the attic, took the stained message of longing and ran down the attic steps, wordlessly running through the fields to ask the evening sky if the world had gone wrong and if it did, why.

Beneath a twisted Sycamore, where the clouds parted against a purple horizon, Daniel held the brittle piece of paper as if he were holding a life, a life worthy of security. The moss-covered trees and the twilight critters began to sing their songs. "Harrison," Daniel whispered. "I miss you so much. My arms are useless without you. No one to hug. No one to wrap my arms around." Speaking out loud did not change the reality of his life, but he felt someone listening. Daniel wondered how many people knew about The Blues Man on Whitman Lane and how long he had been around. "1927," Daniel said. "He's probably an old fart." Daniel rested against the Sycamore for several hours and fell asleep. A sharp sting pulled him out from the stillness of a forgotten reverie. The bugs had chewed him up. "Damn," he said, slapping his arms and scratching the back of his head feverishly.

"You didn't think I'd come," whispered a voice behind him.

It was Harrison, dressed in a pair of blue jeans cut shorts and a tight black shirt. His chest was broad, and his defined pecks and abs pressed against his shirt. Daniel had never seen Harrison look so attractive.

"What are you doing here?"

"Listening," he said.

"To what, man? You traveled an hour across Louisiana to listen?"

"Yes."

"Why?"

"Why not?"

A yellow light illuminated the cracks in Daniel's jeans. He pulled out his cellphone, glared at his mother's urgent message and hurled the phone to the ground. "Are you ready or what?" With his strong, muscular arms folded across his chest, Harrison grinned. The whiteness of his teeth in the dark reminded Daniel how much he wanted him, how much he would give him, how easily he could tackle him to the ground and drain him. "I've been waiting for weeks, Harrison." They held each other under the dark sky, pressing their warm bodies together and a sense of erotic relief lifted from the both of them as they kissed. Daniel's teeth caught Harrison's bottom lip, pulling it and, without warning, releasing it. Daniel relaxed his head against Harrison's pounding heart.

"Come on," Harrison said. "Let's go see him."

"Would you make fun of me if I told you I'm scared?"

"Not in a million years."

In the sinister darkness, where the ghosts of slaves could still be heard singing below uprooted trees, Daniel and Harrison followed a narrow dirt path cut across a ghostly clearing and found a road. "Whiteman Lane?" Harrison tried to see through the night. "Don't see any signs around here. We're alone, Dan."

"It's strange to be so far away and yet so close. We are alone. So, he's got to be one old, tough man. You don't think he'll..." Daniel paused, listened to the crickets, and kicked the rocks on the road.

"Shoot us?" Harrison said.

"Yeah. I was going to say that."

"No. He's one of those old fashion types. I heard all about him in New Orleans. They say he sits in a rocking chair on his front porch, waiting for Satan to come along so he can kill him with his guitar. If you're not Satan, you don't have anything to worry about."

"Fiddlesticks," Daniel whispered. "I can see him now, waiting for us to come along, holding a shotgun in one hand and a guitar in the other. 'Boys,' he'd say, 'No business being up in these parts.' I'd die."

"We're not turning back. We found this paper for a reason. He can help us."

"All right."

Daniel had rented Woodstock a few years ago and enjoyed it. Richie Havens performed first. The sound of Haven's guitar had filled Daniel with passion, an unknown passion for music. After Richie walked out on stage, violently strumming the strings on his guitar, the hippies in the audience were hypnotized by the guitar's magnetism. Both Harrison and Daniel heard the sound of a guitar through the bent branches along the road similar to Haven's, exciting the toads along the ponds, commanding the birds to sleep, and pulling the boys closer and closer to a man who they had believed would shoot them with a shotgun. A small, wooden cabin appeared at the end of Whitman Lane. An orange glow blanketed the windows. The shadow of a man sitting in a chair on the front porch almost stopped Daniel's heart. "I see him," he whispered.

"And I see you," shouted The Blues Singer. "I see many things out there in the dark. Things move, dance, skip or just die. It depends on the day, I guess. I thought I'd see you boys sooner, but life always gets in the way of the most important things. That's how it goes. Get on up here."

The boys cautiously approached the man in the shadows. The orange light revealed a withered old black man with a six-string guitar. His hands were as black as oil, stretched and tired. His long face, covered with scars and deep wrinkles changed as the orange light from the windows danced. Daniel thought he could hear the crackling of a fire and whispers inside. "We found this piece of paper," Harrison stuttered.

"I know. I sent it. I send them out all over. Some of them have washed up along the coast of New Zealand, wherever that is. That's just what I've been told." The Blues Singer laughed. "Well, I'll tell you what, I've got a few songs left in me and I'd like for you to listen. Can you do that for me, a tired old man with the blues?"

"Why do you have the blues?"

"I don't have the blues, son, the blues has me. Now, sit down there and listen."

The Blues Singer lifted his right arm, strummed a chord and the darkness vanished behind them. A bright red glow filled the spaces between the trees. Shadows walked through the blaze. They were tall, skinny, and singing along with The Blues Singer. His voice, almost touched by supernatural grace, shook their hearts. "Don't the moon look lonesome, shinin' through the trees? Don't the moon look lonesome, shinin' through the trees?" The words fell from his mouth with such sheer fervor. Daniel's eyes watched as his fingers danced along the guitar, hitting notes, slamming chords, and recreating a scene that haunted and inspired long before they were knee high to a grasshopper.

The music stopped. The red glow died. Shadows returned to their graves. "Those are my relatives, folks that once lived and breathed just like you. Now, they're off on their own. Walkin' that place that we all lived before. For every ghost in that darkness, I have given a gift."

Daniel thought he should be afraid of the peculiar man, but the feeling was silenced by the music. The Blues Singers told the boys to open his front door and look inside. Harrison pushed open the door and saw hundreds and hundreds of guitars. They were all glowing.

"Every guitar in there is a ghost," he said. "Some keep me up at night, others simply don't bother me. They glow, they sing along, and they know what has happened to them. Shut the door, boy." Harrison reached for the knob, pulled the door shut and stared at Daniel.

"They're souls," Harrison said. "You promise them things in life and in return you..."

141

The Blues Singer chuckled. "Shut up. You've got to understand a few things about a few things." The boys laughed. "Laugh, go ahead. You need to realize that I made a deal long ago at the crossroads and now I'm just doing my part. What do you want?"

Daniel pulled Harrison by the arm and whispered in his ear. "I'm not sure about this. Let's go."

"Are you willing to share one lifetime with me in exchange for having your soul live in a guitar forever?" Harrison's words were spoken with anger.

"I am." Daniel replied.

Harrison admired the silver rings on The Blues Singer's hands, stepped up to the rocking chair and cleared his throat. "I want to spend the rest of my life with him. Can you make that happen?"

The Blues Singer nodded. "Young kids and their funny ways. Well, we had folk like that back then, too. I can do that."

"Like what?" Harrison asked.

The Blues Singer raised his eyebrows. "It takes all types to make the world spin."

Daniel Patterson and Harrison Steele walked away from The Blues Man holding hands. They felt different. It was a different kind of feeling inside their bones. As they looked back at the shack, Daniel stopped and instructed Harrison to look up. "Look," Daniel said. "That's the most fascinating thing I've ever seen."

Harrison tilted his head and felt his heart flutter in his chest. "I agree. Never seen anything like it. Come on."

They passed a sign that read: Guitars for Sale, The Blues Man's Place.

Within a Dark Wood
(Inspired by Hansel and Gretel)

They were standing near a basement window, gazing across a field blanketed in whiteness only familiar to the coldness of December and the wintery mix of ice and snow forced the trees to lean as if they, too, could not endure the coldness of a winter storm. Brother and sister, both sincere in their peculiar imaginative nature, were living with a father who consumed more bottles of whiskey than the local drunkard in town and a stepmother who loathed them because they were not her own children. These children, with their deep brown eyes and chestnut colored hair, were growing weary of their stepmother who, without any impartial origin, forced them to sleep on a cold, stone floor in the basement of the small, wooden cottage their father had built years ago. A dilapidated barn, rising out from behind the cottage, forced the children to confront their fate.

"We're like that barn," Charles said to his sister one day. "We're just here. One day, we're gonna end up looking just like that old barn."

Joni, who appeared to be taller than her brother, grinned and placed her hand on his shoulder to comfort his fear of being lost in the dense hills of their father's dismal nightmare. "We'll never be like that barn, Charlie. We're better than that. Remember what momma used to tell us? 'You're angels without wings, walking the woods to protect what is your own. Never forget who you are.' So, don't fear." They sat together in the basement, stumbling over memories that spoke of things their father had forgotten or perhaps buried somewhere beneath the soil of the cottage. A doorknob twisted in the darkness, summoning fear from both Charles and Joni. "I hear you little brats down there whispering about me. No dinner tonight. Wish your father would throw you away." The door slammed shut and the children wept in the darkness of their own sorrow.

Sorrow is not for children. Sorrow is for people who are prepared for it, who understand its endless twists and turns like the woods outside. Charles and Joni held each other as the snow drifted through the warped limbs of lonely trees. "We're leaving tonight," Charles told Joni. "We can't stay here anymore. No one knows us. We're like unknown people. We can run away together, find a new life, a new world to treat us better."

"I don't know," Joni uttered, shaking her head. "What'll happen to father? What if that wicked stepmother of ours finds us? She'll peel the skin from our bones and feed us to her garden. I'm scared."

"Being afraid is what it's all about, Joni. If you don't fear, how else are you gonna know where to go or where to place your feet?"

Joni thought for a few moments and smiled. "I believe we could escape through the basement window when it's dark. You know how the bitch upstairs hates the darkness."

Charles nodded.

Joni started up again with a pure and accurate plan. "Once it's dark and everyone's asleep, we'll crawl out from the basement window and run to the woods. We won't look back."

"Yes," whispered Charles, looking up at the door where the form of their stepmother often stood. "We'll do it."

Charles and Joni decided that night to escape from the disconnected world they were born into. Only a farmer, who lived miles and miles away, had told them about schools and buses and classrooms, places where children were taught by adoring teachers and made friends. It all appeared to be a dream to Charles and Joni as they listened to him. The farmer spoke of a fast-moving world, dominated by cruel leaders and boxes with screens on them that informed people about all kinds of things. Even if such a world would never appeal to Charles and Joni, they would find it in their hearts to locate a home of peace and joy. Contentment did not exist at the cottage with their father and stepmother. No ideas or songs or thoughts were ever openly expressed. Silence and obedience were the laws of their stepmother.

In the night, when the clouds rolled back over the hills and the wolves howled at its beauty, Charles and Joni lifted the basement window and crawled out. Motionless in the shadows, almost mutilated by the idea of fear, Charles pulled Joni's arm and they ran across the field and into the darkness where animals screamed out at nature's enigmatic splendor. "We have to run fast," said Joni, glaring back at the cottage. "Come on, hurry!"

Their feet crunched leaves, cracked twigs, and stumbled over icy puddles and broken tree limbs. A silver glow illuminated their path as if the moon knew Charles and Joni's pain. They followed the glow, often jumping at the sounds in the darkness, breathless and tired by memories of their stepmother and their sorrow for their father. Nothing could be done. How could it? Their father had watched them suffer endlessly as their stepmother punished them by slamming their fingers in cabinets, starving them, and whipping them with leather belts. It all had to change. Everything.

Charles and Joni knew pain and sorrow more so than any other child in the area. Such a fear inspired them to venture into the woods to find a new world. The woods were far more than a thick wooded labyrinth of trepidation. The trees resembled freedom and the darkened landscapes punctured Charles and Joni's soul as they traveled through the ominous curled branches of isolated trees. Charles and Joni's hunger began to weaken their ability to walk.

"Perhaps we can travel in the morning," Charles said, as he rested against a tree. "We've walked through these woods for hours. Haven't seen a thing. No sounds of childish laughter, no cars or airplane's in the sky. The stars are covered by the clouds."

Joni sat next to her brother. "The moon is coming through, Charlie. We've got enough light to find our way home if we have to. I don't mind at all. In fact, I'd rather poison our stepmother with the arsenic sitting at the top of the basement."

Charles shook his head. "No. Bad idea. We're so far and we can't turn back now. Momma used to say that we should remember who we are. We're not servants, Joni. We are not turning back!"

"Okay," Joni whispered sadly. "We'll travel deeper into the woods, although we've certainly lost our way. I trust you. I guess we have no other choice."

They had decided their fate. There was no room for fear in the house of beauty and imagination they had built years ago. They sat beneath the tree for several hours, observing the unidentified shadows coiled beneath the trees. The woods were a haunted place. Everyone knew it. Charles and Joni were quite familiar with the ghosts in the woods and the legends they were told by their father. He once told Charles and Joni that a strange woman lived deep in the woods, a woman who chopped up little children and consumed their flesh and meat to preserve her youthfulness. Such legends were whispered by local farmers and woodsmen who traveled through the cottage telling tales of ghost trains and Ezra Pound and Woody Guthrie.

Times had changed. There were no more storytellers other than the ones who had lived far away and those stories often reflected a horrific hobo condition. Stories of moonshiners and outdoor woodsmen echoed throughout the hills. The children, locked away in a cold basement, would press their ears against the basement door and listen to their father as he explained the specific locations to recover gasoline, food, and other goods.

These whispers were a rare and frequently surprising occurrence. The children were not allowed to read books. Their deceased mother had taught them how to read and write at a very early age. After their mother's death and their stepmother occupied their mother's bed, things changed. They always did; whether one would like them to or not.

Charles and Joni walked for hours and hours in the darkness of the woods. A limestone building, cuddled by lifeless vines and darkened windows welcomed them. Although the curved roof and the broken entrance nearly inspired Joni to turn away, Charles could smell cinnamon, coffee, onions and freshly baked bread. Together Charles and Joni listened to their growling stomachs and decided to knock on the door and ask for shelter. The winter storms were a part of their upbringing. Snow, ice, chilly wind drifts, numb fingers, and reddened faces were not uncomfortable to the children. Winter was a bitch and they never dared to disrespect the seasons or the land they had roamed and explored for years and years.

Charles knocked on the wooden door. The splintered wood in the door revealed bright lights and a flickering flame.

"I'm cold and hungry," Joni whispered with chattering teeth. A cloud of cold breath from Joni's lips convinced Charles that he had no other choice. They had walked for hours and hours and the sun was still hiding. Being far away from home fills one's body with recollection and nostalgia. But, as Charles knocked on the door and peered at his sister Joni with sympathetic eyes, he could not turn away. If they were going to escape the insufferable brutality of their stepmother, they would have to ask for shelter and food occasionally. What else were they going to do?

As Charles knocked, Joni examined the darkness of the house. The arched windows were filled with the flickering flames of warmth; she could help but find such a house to be inviting and consoling. Joni, with her short-sleeved blouse and jeans shook as the wind caressed her hair. Charles, who detested sweaters, wore a hoodie with a sports team logo. New Orleans Saints? Who knew? Goosebumps pulled themselves to the surface of Joni's arms as she watched a shadow appear in the doorway. The children were pleased by the appearance of a withered old woman with silver hair and deep dark eyes. Her skin looked like paper, thin and wrinkled.

Her smile, crooked and sinister did not run the children off, for they spoke quietly in the winter air of their stepmother, their father's fate, and their destination. The old woman, draped in a cobweb robe, listened to the children as they spoke about their lives and their abusive stepmother. "She wouldn't feed us for days and days," Joni explained. "We slept on a cold floor in the basement with no lights, no food, and no mattress. Nothing. And poor Charlie would often take my side and she'd slam his fingers in the cabinets for punishment. I can't take it anymore. I know you do not know us or even understand what's going on. But, please, we need shelter and food and warmth."

The old woman nodded with eyes of compassion and allowed both Charles and Joni to join her in a heated, sandalwood scented room with old candles, books, dust, and cobwebs. The floorboards moaned beneath the children's weight. A cat, somewhere upstairs, meowed and scuttled across the hall and vanished into a dark room. The living room made Charles and Joni feel safe. The fire warmed their flesh. The old woman's sincere, aged smile weakened Joni's fear of nearly everything. No fear. The thoughts she had circling her mind about her stepmother vanished and she thought about her mother and her words. Nothing mattered. Keep yourself safe. Stay together. Find or build a sanctuary. Joni was often overwhelmed by such thoughts, although she did not allow such thoughts to define her and Charles' disposition.

The old woman was wordless as she wandered into the kitchen and fed the children bacon, ham, fresh bread, and milk. Charles' eyes were filled with a sea of questions, but he did not wish to interfere with the old woman's peculiar quietness and unusual behavior. Of course, Charles and Joni thought about the rumors of the old woman who lived deep in the woods and ate children. It could not have been her, Joni thought. Her home, adorned with cheap prints of Van Gough and Monet, made the environment appear harmless, almost like a real home. She offered the children to sleep in one of the bedrooms upstairs with two beds that smelled of cotton and fresh cold breezes.

The old woman ignited a fire in the fireplace and disappeared. Charles rested on his bed and watched as Joni pulled the sheets back. "Is she the witch?" Joni whispered. "What if she's the old woman that farmer was talking about?"

Charles wrinkled his brow with concern. "That farmer said the old woman was a cannibal, ate children and hikers. Know how many people went missing in these woods in last ten years? Dozens. Most of them were children. How can an old lady do all that?"

Charles comforted Joni's fear and she sighed with relief. "It was nice of her to let us in. She didn't ask many questions and neither did we. I see she doesn't have electricity like some of the folks up in the hills. Well, we're gonna rest well tonight. Remember, Charles, no fear."

The Children slept, soundless during the night. They wrestled with strange dreams of their stepmother running after them through the woods with a knife. They had walked for miles and miles and wandered through the woods at night for hours and hours. They were far away from home. But, the poignant ghosts of the old cottage never left their minds as they slept and dreamed. The sun leaked through the windows the next morning, revealing a small, wooden room warmed by a fire stricken the night before by the old woman. It was a new day. The children were excited and yet overwhelmed by the travelling aroma of freshly baked cinnamon rolls, bacon, and sausage. "We're in the land of paradise, oh yeah, I feel it. Smell that?" Charles pulled the sheet from his body and jumped from the bed.

"Yes," Joni said. "It smells wonderful. I wish we didn't have to leave so soon. I'd rather stay here, help the old lady around the house, and help with meals and things. You, Charles, could help her with her garden and building."

"Are we far enough from father and stepmother to live here unseen? And what if the old woman turns us in or tells us no, we cannot stay here? Then what, huh?"

Joni sighed and folded her arms over her breasts. "If you never try you'll never know. We'll go downstairs and see what's going on."

A black cat, who could have been watching them all night long as they slept and dreamed, guided them down an aged wooden hallway adorned with faded yellow wallpaper. And, for one hurried moment, Charles thought he had seen faces in the wallpaper, watching him and sister as they followed the cat downstairs. The old lady must have heard the sounds of children's feet on the steps, for her, after preparing breakfast, lurked behind the banister and smiled.

"Hope you slept well," the old woman said with her eyes following her black cat. "He's a guardian. Come into the kitchen and sit down."

Her voice was like an out of tune piano found in an abandoned mansion somewhere in the dense hills of nowhere. She spoke softly and the warmth of her words filled the children with hope. They sat together around an old wooden table and began eating cinnamon rolls with vanilla icing, bacon, and sausage rolls. Saliva dripped from the corner of Charles' mouth. He had never tasted such goodness in all of his life. Spices brought euphoria to his tangled observations of the old woman's house. "I don't want to know your names or where you came from or how you got here. I don't like questions and questions don't like me. I've lived on this land since I was born. I've watched all of my family die here and they're all in the back."

Joni turned around to look out the kitchen window. She could see a few ashen stones scattered out in the yard. There was a beautiful clearing before the kitchen door. Dead golden vines encircled the railing of the porch. It was more than pleasant for Joni to see. "So, I don't expect any straight answers from you kids. I just want to help. I'm not out to get you, but I believe there's someone else out to get you."

Charles and Joni looked down and nodded. They stopped eating. "Yes," Charles said. "We escaped my father's house far away. Our stepmother will kill us both if we should return."

"You speak very well for such a young boy," the old woman said. "You must have been educated at home, away from public schools and all that."

"Correct," Joni said. "We've never been to a city or even a small, remote town. We're traveled the trails and spoke to woodsmen who told us stories of the modern world. Have you seen it?"

156

The old woman rolled her eyes as if she had been confronted with the authority of a sincere questioning. "Yes," she whispered, leaning over the table and looking into Joni's eyes. "You have no idea what's going on out there. No idea at all and I'd never wish you to see it. Let me put it to you kids this way, if you go out there, in the real world as they call, the place of opportunity and friends and employment and all the other nonsense that makes people sick of being what they are, you end up losing yourself in some unseen way."

Charles and Joni did not quite understand what the old woman spoke of. But, they feared the chaos beyond their land. "Don't look so frightened, child. You're going to be just fine. No one knows you're here. Right?"

Charles and Joni nodded their heads. "We're all alone."

"Well, I'll hide you two as long as I can. But, I know I haven't had anyone knock on my door in well over a decade so I believe the chances of such a thing occurring is highly unlikely. How do you like your breakfast?"

"Oh, it's splendid," shouted Charles. "Delicious."

The old woman appeared to be pleased and cleaned the tables and washed the dishes and glared out her window to see if anyone was going to come up the trail. She wanted to help the children and she provided room and board for them as long as they made their beds, finished up dishes, and hand washed their own clothes.

After several months had passed, Charles and Joni ventured into the old woman's basement more out of curiosity than in search of anything in particular. While looking at the canned goods on a long line of shelves on a far, dark wall, Charles spotted what looked like an old door. He opened it easily and as his eyes adjusted to this dim, small room—lit only by two cloudy windows—he spotted a pile of bones in the left corner. Bloodied flannel shirts, boots, hats, and other miscellaneous items were stored here. Newspaper clippings displaying the faces of missing children and local hikers covered the walls. The room—this surprising find—was a chamber of alarming cruelty. "They're human bones," Charles argued with Joni. "They're human. I don't know what to do, but we've got to get out of here."

Joni examined the articles of clothing covered in blood and squinted her dark eyes at the piles of bones. "They're definitely human. Look, we need to get out of here before she finds out we found the door and all this horror."

"Horror," the old woman whispered as she stepped into the room. "The horror is everywhere, children. The world, the one you seek and wish to be in love with is a world that will only reject you. Yes, these are human bones and yes I did kill them and yes I never wanted to hide it from either of you. I wouldn't eat either of you if the winds of time asked me herself. No. Pure children you are, almost divine and hopeful. My own soul can only eat those with wicked hearts or bad souls. I've grown weak for months, for human flesh preserves my beauty. If I would eat a pure soul, my skin would break and my bones would melt and my eyes would burst. You see, I am different. I'm not gonna put you in an oven and eat you. No. I need a rotten soul, a spirit that tortures those who want love. I eat people who are savage, people who put money over love, power over compassion, hatred over love. I have lived here for many years and the bones of these souls and the newspaper clippings along the walls define a perfectly just execution. I've helped many travelers find their way home. I've fed children who were lost. I feed the birds, nurture the garden, and kiss the flowers while they are prospering. I'm growing weaker by the day."

"So you only eat evil people," Joni asked, feeling her heart pounding against her chest. "Only bad people?"

"That's right. Nature has a way of killing things off as they should be, just as she has a way of bringing things to life as they should be.

Beyond these hills, over the small towns and rivers, I would be a witch or a monster or some kind of fairytale creature that eats children. Honestly, I adore older men."

The old woman chuckled as the children stared at her. "Anyhow, I'm older now and things have to change. I can't do it myself anymore. I'm weak and hungry. I need a wicked soul to eat. Do you know of anyone? It'll remove over five decades of wrinkles and in exchange for your offering; I'll teach you children the ways of the craft and how to live forever. And, you'll be able to see your father again."

Charles and Joni looked at each and smiled. "Yes," they both shouted. "We know someone really well. Our stepmother lives several leagues beyond the creek and over the river. My father is a gentle man. Go find her and bring her back to us all alive."

The old woman grinned. "First, I'm gonna do everything to her as she has done to you. Then, we'll have some more fun. Children, watch over the house tonight. I'll be traveling with my feline who tells me when it's not safe and I'll travel over the creek and locate the cottage. Your father will be unharmed and he'll never know I was even there. Afterwards, both of you can dance back to your father's house with joy as long as you visit me every now and again. I loathe old age."

A plan had been made. Shadows danced against the walls as the orange glow of the fire chased things that weren't even there. The children locked the doors to the old woman's house and watched as she floated through the mist around the trees and the cat followed. "Stepmother," the children whispered. "Now it's your turn."

The Somewhat Invisible Ghost

To the discontented dreams walking through the dismal decadence of a generation's misplaced sincerity, along the corners of empty markets and abandoned townhouses and drug-infested parks and housing projects, the blanket of eternity warms the contemporary chills of sadness along a stranger's spine—

To the soulful singers and the tired poets, the dreamers, idealists, and the hobos whose dust clings to the ghost engines of locomotives of Southern melancholia, along the thickets of thorns coated with the blood of the Negroes and their unchanged magic and blood-soaked karma, the America we know must confront such chilling histories—

To the woeful songs of the youth, spilling across the timeless waves of devolution and unspoiled shores of lost memory, the melodies churn with thunder within the basin of toxic sewage and the lifeless poets dare to dream the dream no man can find satisfying—

To the sun and the moon, the two entities in the sky passing by the horror all eyes wish to pierce with flame and melt the plastic Hollywood images of our time, with the serrated edge of a knife's blade flickering like a silver jewel in the moonlight, where Hamlet's laughter stimulates the rhythm of consciousness like the quickened excitement of a perfected sonnet to the empty epiphany brain of our reckless care—

To the mothers who long to smother their little boys and girls with the cradle palm and the warm breast, for her eyes weep at the chaos with folded arms and crooked necks, and to gaze at the unemployment lines are to follow the coiled stems of the snakes and the thieves, the politicians and their two-faced theories—

To the fathers who have lost their fathers to chance or depravity, to the neglected sons whose hearts must pump concrete with panic, their soccer balls and toy guns have yet to be touched by the jolt of masculinity as the father climbs his mountain of abandonment and carelessly invokes the same demons that destroyed his father—

To the lonesome drunkards, the feverish crack dealers, the dismal meth-heads, and the 9 to 5 dead-end workers, I shall greet them with a glass of enlightenment and reason, but their skin is far too thick to be punctured with the spike that shimmers on Liberty's head—

To my generation of apathy, how unchanged the afterlife must be, for you know nothing of oblivion but you know everything about the technologically advanced systems of dishonesty, you utilize such things to mask your insecurities and dismal glares and vacant grins and fake smiles, but we pray for you in Time magazine and the newspapers hate both of us—

To the madness in every age, that horrid illness that touches the infant and the elder, that rapes the virgin and the whore, and pushes time and stops it, we have crawled far into the prison cell to escape the shadows that are our shadows—

To the innocence splattered on the sidewalk, the blood flows imagination twisted, images of the worse kind, marketed and packaged by the hands of those who work mindlessly in the factories of tyranny, who have wept at the clock longer than the clock has wept at them—

Who have played the guitar with bloody fingertips and poured truckloads of sweat into their musical dreams as the mirrors on the walls reflected a howling skeleton beyond the gates of Eden, who have slept with friends and a friend of a friend as the world turned them against each other by a simple twist of time—

Who have challenged the social order with a gesture or a pen or a bullet as the world broke out against the police and the Pagan feasts, those ragged Bleeker Street dwellers that mopped the Village with bloody hands and hopeful poetry, Simon and Garfunkel's Sparrow died because of them, those misguided souls that turn their face from the bum who remind them of themselves more than their own reflection, bones, and mistakes—

Whose false impression we are admiring on the vacant walls of impossibility, where the nurturer and the wicked stepmother run circles around the fiction of truth and the books you shall never read but read anyway—

Who have walked the road no one else would walk, but crawled as they talked and walked as they barked beneath the haunted turns of memory wooded wandering, therein lies the hollowed caverns of abyss, the holes within you that turn out to be true, truer and finer than anything you could do—

Who have fought in the wars called upon by the unbearable static currents, those who have lost ears, eyes, fingers, and legs, the wheelchair bound poet in his muted expression, the condemned man and the electric chair, to the barber, teacher, priest, judge and his wife—

To the children at school and the dancing childless fool, who have witnessed death passing by, the lovers and isolated writers, even the aunt and uncle who sigh, we watch, we eat, we challenge what we greet, and the nameless shall remain nameless through the obscured faces of the shameless—

Undertakers reveal their hidden identities as the wealthy man's child wanders in confusion, to the traveling blues men who have sold the man in the long black coat more than a few songs and strained strings of struggling strumming sorrow—

Painless pandemonium within the pipe-dreaming poets, who have watched houses burn in haunted hapless hoping, but the Nun knows not to place her loyalty with the pimp and the sinful nature of our universe—

To the weakened hearts and the heavy souls, to the oversaturated handkerchiefs and the pain very few shall ever know, who have promised the great promise on a lonesome night and waited up for the end of the world as the world ended them—

Who have waited for assurance on the front of the daily newspapers, it is the soundlessness of ignorance that writes all these papers, and the ink reads black, glazed, political, right, left, middle, left, right—

To the editors in chief and the homeless firetrap, to the wrinkled feet caught on nails throughout America's chest, the dreamers have dreamed and you shall all wake, to the findings of truth on every corner, to epiphany's immortal idealized intelligence, the poetry written on dead-end walls and the forgetful shall remember what was lost—

This intoxicating fume of poetry caught, the flame of predication, and all that assuming has deeply wrought.

The Abortionist's Crime

Sirens explode from the city streets below. Milk cartons tumble down vacant alleyways, chasing pieces of newspaper with forgotten obituary names in an unnoticed wind. The world is burning and no one can put the fire out. Traces of misery are left spray painted along uneven brick walls. Voices of poetic musings are either demolished by the city or are left to be muffled by the procession of junkies and local misfits who crawl through the subterranean poems of the city without an upward glance. Most of these fiends wrestle with their needles and bundles of cash, moist from nervous hands, swearing helplessly in the night of heroin madness.

I have known this city longer than I have known myself. Visions of a different world have left me trembling with both apprehension and indecision. Who needs a better world? What does that mean, anyway? Do I want it? America is standing along the edge of an ill-omened precipice, looking down at waters filled with the faces of her own children and she laughs. Yes, she laughs as if it is the last image of morbid comedy she will ever see or pretend to understand.

I have been shooting up for nearly five years. The walls of my haunted apartment, once inviting and adorned with blossoming magnolias, is now stale and discolored by perpetual smoking and greasy hands. I have a mattress on the floor, a wrecked air-conditioner filled with roaches, and an empty refrigerator with a severed cord. I have lived alone for over three years, sleeping with my arms reaching out for someone to hold, smoking with no voice to speak to my wandering mind, and drinking to prevent my brain from bleeding. It doesn't help that my neighbor is a prostitute. She's one of those helpless girls who yearns for her father's embrace, smothering her idiocy with semen and beer. When I check the mail, I'll often see her peaking at me through her cracked door. I helped her. Yes, I did.

Her eyes, darkened with depravity and bitterness, understands that I don't care about her or what she does. She understands my addiction just as much as I understand hers. She's beautiful, too. With shameful brown eyes and a guitar-shaped frame, she reminds me of everything I wish I could care about but can't.

Some nights, when the sounds of life outside die down, I'll lie on my mattress and feel the euphoria in my blood running away like a devious woman who knows she's crossed the line. "Come back," I'll say, "I'm not finished." She'll turn, grin, and whisper, "I'm too dangerous for you." I want to tell her it's already too late. I'm in. I'm stuck. I'm addicted. She doesn't care. She never does. With a few groans and a bottle of wine, I'll try to make sense of where I am or where I'm going. I'll think about the family I left behind in the Mid-West. They're all dead now.

I'll shoot up a second time close to midnight, tickling my nightmares into perfected dreams and gaze at the ceiling, somewhere between the silhouettes of my baby toys and the ghosts of my parents rattling chains near the cracked windows that look out at desolation or a stage, I'm not sure which. Somewhere, someone is crying. It's me.

We're so apathetic here in this fucking city. Too tired to care, too tired to cry, too tired to believe in something more than what we see every day on the streets or in the newspapers or along the sidewalks filled with businessmen and corporate rats with rebellious children, and inside the homes with medicine cabinets filled with everything from Benzedrine to opiates. Yes, their children know where to look. The babies make me cry. I see them all the time. They're crawling around in dumpsters where their mothers left them, stuck to metal and plastic. I'll turn away from them every chance I get because that's what we do here. That's America.

Occasionally, I'll remember a time when someone gave a shit and the thought walks out the door just as soon as it had walked in. "Interesting," I'll say, "I remember shit like that. I wonder if anyone else remembers a little thing called love." My eyes will see a Dylan concert poster, touring with Baez and I'll laugh. "Those were the days." Were they really? Nothing is more worthy of remembrance than those you love. I used to have someone to love. I did. I used to kiss her goodnight and make her breakfast. She was my baby. But she died.

She was pregnant with my child. Her happiness was enough to keep the sickness of addiction away. If I'd see her smile in the mornings, I knew I wouldn't go out and get my fix. It kept the demons of guilt as far away from me as possible. But, she found junk, too. Our baby died. She blamed me. After she killed herself, I struggled to forget about everything. Her overdose was my overdose. The world stopped moving. I never open the closet door where she wanted to die. She's still there. If smelling her decaying corpse is the only thing I can keep from her, I will. I made that decision a longtime ago. I'm sure nothing is left except for hair and bones. It's been years. But, there are moments when I'll still catch a whiff of her. No one should know this.

When you've been enslaved to a substance for so long, you become paranoid, delusional, moody, careless in your thinking and pro-foundly nostalgic. Addiction takes all your mistakes, tears, and weaknesses and forces them to be okay with your troubled mind. The truth is, it's not okay. In fact, it's a blend of everyone's weariness and sorrows and you feel it crash against the shores of your heart. Why am I so receptive, you'll think? Why does this have to happen to me? The truth crawls through your marrow, eating your insides like some parasite. No one gives a flying shit if this is happening to you and that's why you keep doing it, to make yourself feel truly loved by something and not someone.

I wonder what would happen if I told the police I had my dead lover's body in the closet of my apartment, too afraid to open it. Her eyes find me when I'm high. "Jesus Christ," I'll scream, "What are you doing here? What do you want from me? You left me! You left me! You left me! I don't love you anymore."

Her rotting flesh will fall to the floor with a smack, collecting coagulated blood to reflect my sorrowful eyes. She knows I'm not her lover now. "Open the closet door and let me go," she'll plead. "It's dark and lonely in there."

"No."

"Why?"

"Bitch!"

"Why?"

"I can't."

No one remembers her name. No one. I don't. It's lost in a box filled with unpaid bills and receipts from our days in the Village. Someone called for her a month or two after she died. I never returned the call. After removing the phone line and throwing all the address books away, I figured no one would ever care about her and I was right. Yes, I'm always right. But, I'm always wrong and I know why.

My dealer, Craig, is the only man in the city who knows how I feel. He's a loan officer and pushes more heroin out of his office than the residents of Acapulco. He's currently responsible for seventeen deaths in the last year. Sometimes I forget his name, other times I remember it because I feel like it's the last name I'll ever know. This drug, which remains in my veins, is everything Craig warned me it would be. He's an overconfident, green-eyed type of character from those mobster films from the early 1940s. Some days he's Vladimir Nabokov and other days he's a preacher. He prides himself on how many people he's responsible for killing. "They buy it, man," he attempts to explain with a toothpick in his mouth, "Cash in hand. I don't care what happens to them once they're out of my sight. As long as I've got the cash, they're just another piece of shit junkie."

Craig's young. Anyone from the street can see Craig's fear. He's afraid of everything around him and the junk he pushes out of his business. What a cheap trickster he is! I told him about the death of my lover, the woman suffering from eternal sleep in the closet and he frowned and puffed on his cigarette. "What? Are you fucking crazy? You're telling me your girlfriend's dead in the closet? What in the hell is wrong with you?"

"Trying to figure it out, man. Don't get hung up on this. I've got everything under control."

"Yeah, I can see that you dumbass. Someone's going to call the police. Hell, the smell will be enough to wake herself back up from the dead."

"Both apartments are empty."

"Bitch across the hall?"

"Busy. Too busy to care about the stench of a rotting corpse."

"Damn. I don't know what to say."

"How about nothing."

"You need to get your shit together, man. I remember when you'd come down to the Gaslight and hangout. Do you still write poetry?"

"No poetry here, man. Only grief."

"Damn. I got to go."

I don't see Craig around these days. For some odd reason or another, I feel like I've killed more people than Craig. I've got over a hundred dead, screaming babies haunting me. On a good day, I'll see three or four crawling across the floor, dragging umbilical cords across the black and white checkered floor. I'll glance at them, grin, and cry. I've cried enough tears to fill a lake. Years ago, I performed home abortions for those unfortunate girls from Columbia University. Some days, I'd have a housewife who had an affair or a teacher who feared abrupt termination for being pregnant. These women were kind and sincerely overwhelmed with sadness.

Those who knew my name were told to forget it after the procedures were done. Never fully trusting males, I'd inform the women to leave their husbands or their affairs outside by the sidewalk. For a junkie, these things were never easy to do. But, I'd often wish to die after I performed an abortion.

"You don't have an obligation to these women," my lover once said. "They're just women, crying over the most trivial things. You don't have to do this."

"I have to. Who else will help them?"

Don't judge me so damn harshly. If you could have seen the faces of these women who would walk up to me and weep on my chest, you'd have to consider it, right? Their stories of heartache and abandonment were enough to torture any soul who dared to venture so far into the underground city. So many things happen here. Doctors are junkies. Lawyers are drug-dealers.

Poets are madmen. This is your America, not mine. My America is sweet as a hive of honeybees, a thousand ugly stings and a monotonous hum of discontent forces my addiction to junk to yield before the feet of America. No one bothers me when I'm straight. With trembling fingers and a sweaty brow, my eyes dance across unfamiliar faces with fluttering eyelids. As soon as I feel the warmth in my blood and my mind drifts with the absurd high of junk, someone will knock on the door, the sounds of sirens are caught between buildings, and the world jumps in. Hell. That's what it is to me, Hell.

A few nights ago, the whore from across the hall found me standing near her mailbox, dazed and paranoid. I never take the mail up. I let it pile up. Somehow, I managed to pay my rent. I'd rather shoot up in my apartment than in some back alley where groups of damaged heroin addicts huddle together like a patched quilt. She was crying, the whore was crying.

"Another day in paradise," she mumbled, whipping tears from her eyes. "I think this place is getting to me."

"I used to be different," I told her, closing the lid to the mailbox. "I thought I'd soar above the madness. Nope."

"Why are you still here?"

"Sometimes, we'd rather die with our heads hung with shame than go out and make our lives better."

I remember how frightened she was when she asked me to help her with an unfortunate problem. I could feel it coming. I had seen those kind of tears before. The whore, with her darkened eyes, was pregnant. I saw my child's face for the first time since that day! She was laughing at me. Distraught with the fear of being seen with the whore by the mailboxes, I invited her up to the apartment and she sat on the bed and I opened my box of instruments and sighed. The bottle of ether nearly escaped from my hand as I watched her fall asleep. I told myself I'd never do this again. I was wrong. After the procedure, she thanked me and asked about my lover who she hadn't seen in a couple years. "She's dead. Overdose."

"I'm sorry," she said, sitting up slowly on the mattress. "I can't tell you how much I appreciate what you've done here. No one will know, right?"

"Right."

"How long have you been doing this?"

"Too long. Get some rest."

Watching her sleep caused me to dream a dream of sorrow unlike I had ever dreamed before. I saw my little girl, screaming in the arms of my lover. I had done this to them, I thought. I killed both of them. I had told myself she had overdosed for so long I believed it. How? I'm convincing, aren't I? My lover didn't want the child because of her own selfishness. She had imagined the child would absorb all my attention and her jealousy was heartache.

I tried to make things better. The abortion went wrong. I even took a break to shoot up in the middle of the procedure. It was my fault she was gone. Darkness at the break of noon promised another tomorrow. I didn't want it and still don't. Here I am, sleeping in the same apartment as my biggest mistake. Don't we all. This is my crime.

About the Author

Jeffrey L. Buford, Jr. was born in the small riverboat town of Alton, Illinois; Mark Twain territory. After attending Lewis and Clark Community College, he went on to study at Southern Illinois University of Edwardsville.

Mr. Buford plays and teaches piano, guitar, and music theory. When not engaged with his family, Mr. Buford walks along the Mississippi river where he listens to the voices of all those who inspire him from past to present. He also enjoys history, science fiction, philosophy, and classic Hollywood.

Mr. Buford's first book—a tell-all slice-of-life memoir about his challenges of growing up as a young man in the culturally divided Mid-west— was published in 2017. *Out of What Crypt They Crawl* is his first book of fiction.

You can write Mr. Buford at:
writer_man2006@yahoo.com